GERUN, THE HERETIC

Being Excerpts from the Clan-Missionary Chronicles

A Science Fiction Novel

by

WILLIAM MALTESE

The Borgo Press
An Imprint of Wildside Press

MMVII

CONTENTS

ABOUT THE AUTHOR

WILLIAM MALTESE was born in the Pacific Northwest. He has a B.A. in Marketing/Advertising and spent an honorable tour of duty in the U.S. Army, achieving the rank of E-5.

He started his authorial career writing for the men's pulp magazines and has since penned more than 150 books, both fiction and nonfiction. According to queerhorror.com, this included the first gay werewolf novel ever published. He also has written a number of bestselling women's romances under the name "Willa Lambert" for houses such as Harlequin and Carousel, including the internationally acclaimed Harlequin SuperRomance #2 (*Love's Emerald Flame*), which is being reprinted by Wildside Press along with many of his other novels.

He encourages his fans to visit his websites:

www.williammaltese.com
www.myspace.com/williammaltese

CHAPTER ONE

Panrun-Ru: Incinerate the book! For it contains heresy.

Maxlima II: Should not we first run it through complete analysis?

Panrun-Ru: We have run it through all the analysis that need be. I repeat, the contents are heretical.

Maxlima II: But what of the molecular makeup of binding and pages? Aren't we missing out on an opportunity to discover new structural formats?

Panrun-Ru: Advantage-Risk does *not* balance out. In my estimate. In the estimate of the Religio-College. You may, of course, file Ruler Prerogative, section 3-dash-7. But, may I remind you of the consequences if the Telegrine Forum rules against you?

Maxlima II: Incinerate the book! But save the man!

—From transcript IV-4-20,
regarding the book found
in the possession of the man,
Jon Missionary. Jesstic File 14-5-6.

GERUN, THE HERETIC, BY WILLIAM MALTESE

WAS IT KALVIN WHO HAD SUMMONED GERUN to this spot of nothingness on the edge of the escarpment?

At seventeen, Gerun wasn't versed well enough in the mentat-exercises to identify the sender error-free. The signet-circle had been Kalvin's, there was no denying that. Forgery of the intricate maze-image would have been impossible for even the craftsmen in Warluck's employ to duplicate. But what of the contents? Added after Kalvin had somehow been tricked into affixing his signet-circle to the mentat-send?

The rendezvous spot had Gerun worried. It was perfect for an ambush. Cylic blazers could easily weave the area and find the target. Boy today, blistered crust tomorrow! Not a pretty anticipation after having survived three assassination attempts in as many terns. Gerun Missionary had every right to be wary.

Would Kalvin really have risked this spot for a meeting? Kalvin who had three-hundred assassination attempts registered against him since the clandestine purge had been initiated by the Religio-College. Not that the Religio-College even now owned up to them. The assassins had been expensively mind-erased to reveal nothing, even when they failed to self-terminate—as at least twenty had done—upon mission failure. Lately, though, suspecting increasing support among a populace long jealous and suspicious of the Missionary gene mix, the Religio-College *had* become more openly vocal with accusations that Jon Missionary had been as heretical as his book. Living, for a member of the

Missionary clan, had become more and more precarious as the family had dwindled from twenty-
four, at the last rising of the stellar curl around
Kynol-II, to a mere four....

"I'm afraid, there are only us two, now," a voice
said, close by, startling Gerun out of a reverie which
had dangerously lowered his defenses against men-
tat-penetration.

"Kalvin?" His inner senses worked overtime to
collate the voice pattern. Ears alone could be deceptive. The sophisticated mechanics had by Warluck
could duplicate to the flaw-minus-six category.

"You mean you were expecting someone else?"
The quick response indicated no fear on the part of
the sender that Gerun would utilize the additional
dialogue for a speedier verification of origin. In fact,
the resumption of a send so quickly as much as indicated a request for Gerun to confirm before actual
face-to-face confrontation. Apparently, the sender
had no intentions of sneaking up on Gerun, while
obviously knowing the boy was waiting. The
sender's voice register was too audible to be haphazardly thrown. Unless, of course, Warluck's lato-
synes had developed even more sophisticated meth-
ods in their dealings with their assumed enemies.

"Only two of us left?" Gerun swerved into ana-
lyzing content once the Kalvin-ident mode seemed
confirmed. The decline of Missionary clansmen had
already gone from twenty-four to four. Now from
four to two? This existent mind-meld the kind
which could only be achieved between one Missionary and another? Gerun was more confident
now that it *was* Kalvin who was the sender. He was

7

disturbed, though, by what the sent message insinuated.

"We are alone, Gerun," came the reply. The send was clearer as the sender grew closer in the darkness, although there was yet no visible sign or other-than-mentat sounding. "I tried to reach Kors, but the lines were already severed. Maseen's channels were clogged with pain interference, indicating poison of the fiss-six variety. I dared not connect for long, of course, because you and I know how fiss poisons break down mentat and allow tracing. Think how many of us have died via fiss ingests so our secrets could be recorded by our enemies upon our exits."

Beyond the decoded vibrations of his ear, Gerun heard the first outside indication of the approach. Kalvin—if it was Kalvin—was near. Beyond the next boulder, around the next bend, the gravel of a dried stream bed crunching beneath the weight of his feet.

"We could be sitting ducks for Cylic blazers," Gerun said. "Not to mention Mylon-probes turned loose within this darkness."

"But we have been too clever for them at the moment," Kalvin sent. "They believe you have slipped the East Gate for meanderings on the Gran Sea. They have servo-ten units scouting even now. I've been no less clever. They've found my rest-cylinder empty and have followed a false trail to the Gryphis Cave. They ponder, and well they might, the motive of a descendant of Jon Missionary conversing with pagan gods." He chuckled. He was old and could see the humor in the game, even though he saw himself—and probably the boy—as eventual losers. "For the moment, you and I are safe from Cylic blazers and Mylon-probes. Not that we are liable to maintain our safety quotients for long," he added pragmatically.

"Two left," Gerun said aloud, the horror of it well upon him. "Soon not even us two?" Then thought: *what is the fear which sparks this purge?*

"The lone surviving segment of the *Book*," Kalvin answered him, his mentat having once again read even Gerun's thoughts via the sympathetic wave-lengths that had once connected all Missionaries (and still did). Alas, Gerun's abilities to mentat-unite with his kin hadn't had nearly the time to develop as Kalvin's had. This was why Gerun needed to *be told* that his last Uncle and Aunt were no longer among the living, while Kalvin had immediately been tuned to their untimely departures.

"What *book*?" Gerun wanted to know. Yes, he could hear the old man's progression now, coming nearer. Anyway, it registered as an old man's progression. Was it a trick? The world was full of cunning tricksters. If they'd tricked inside the defenses of Uncle Kors and Aunt Maseen, how much more vulnerable a mere boy? Gerun had long suspected his defenses were being fortified from outside. Kalvin supervising Gerun's welfare from the wings?

"Don't underestimate your talents for survival," Kalvin sent, having mentat-overheard. "You saved the day at Chinsore when the water surge broke the containing barriers, and you rode the face of the wave with balance that surprised and confused the secret instigators. And at Ron-ron, what could this old man have done to protect you from the pellets launched from unseen attackers in the hills? You

9

lifted the stieler-sec and dodged so expertly those fiss-tipped missiles that could have ended you with a scratch."

"Fiss-tipped?"

"They told you no, didn't they? For whom but Warluck could afford the expense of dipping three-thousand pellets? Did you count them as they whizzed passed? Three-thousand. A tidy sum flushed down the toilet, considering you so skillfully danced the dodge. I hear they scoured the area for the missing, hoping to soak off the bitterment and use it another day. Unfortunately, they have enough for the two of us without it. The Westicks have grown rich on the death of our clan, brewing the lethal doses that Warluck has purchased with cubes of Tilinian. Warluck has financed a grand enemy in the Westicks. Ironic how they've used their money to amass munitions to be used in a revolution against him."

"He risks strengthening the Westicks to kill us?" Gerun asked. Where did Kalvin get his information? It hinted access to data sources not available to Missionaries. He feared again that this wasn't Kalvin heading in his direction.

"Warluck feels safer in dealing with the Westicks than with *We of the Missionary*," Kalvin sent, ignoring any knowledge that Gerun doubted and was readying his C-gun just in case.

"We offered him a bigger threat than the Westicks?" Gerun asked. "How?"

"A question already answered, my boy," Kalvin chided good-naturedly. "You must better learn to categorize your in-feed of information."

"The *Book*?" Gerun ventured.

GERUN, THE HERETIC, BY WILLIAM MALTESE

"Not the *Book* but a page thereof. Not a complete volume but a portion. Salvaged by Panrun-Ru, *The Incinerator*, from his own ruling to incinerate. Who can know what prompted him to salvage the part? Perhaps, he suspected the day would come when a successor needed incentive against the flowering of heretics. Assuming us the heretics in question."

"The *Book* found with Jon Missionary?"

"One and the same," Kalvin sent. "Would that I had access to but a peek at what powers the *Book* insinuated is ours. How Warluck seemed—seems—to fear that we should find out. Alas, he has been too clever for us. I only uncovered filtered word of the fragment after the purge was well begun. At the time word reached me, Melin was just dead, and I did grieve for him, letting the rumor slip completely before confirmation came much too late to be of help. So many of us dead because of this old man's oversight. Any of us to survive? I so old to be of no real threat should I somehow slip through the final net Warluck pulls around us."

He didn't look old; Gerun confirmed when his grandfather was suddenly there before him. Not old as Gerun's parents had waxed suddenly old upon their return from Wistock Cove where, phsi-phsis insisted, they'd been exposed to rare tempmentum. That had been too early in the purge for accusations. In retrospect, however….

"Yes, killed us one by one, two by two; in the case of Mandarin's family, more brazen yet, wiping out six with a single blow and calling it ignited syphicic gas, having the Power Cor confirm," Kalvin said. "A million in insurance doled out to

11

surviving Bet? A price well spent in order to smoothly terminate six, especially since Bet would so soon follow. Klyrinstok Disease, was it? Oh, to exhume her body, all our poor dead bodies, and count the variants of fiss poisoning still clinging to the last of our remains!"

"There's a way to get the *Book* fragment?" Gerun asked.

"Is there?" Kalvin asked, having mistaken the boy's question for a statement. He quickly realized his mistake, feeling silly that he'd been so desperate as to think the boy might come upon something Kalvin hadn't. "Oh, I see, *you* ask *me*. I answer, no. Not that I haven't tried. I've even gone to *Jursimms*." The last was muted whisper. It wasn't a confession he made lightly. He could see the boy's well-deserved disgust. "The Priest was of no help," he added. "I endangered my soul for a word."

"Word?" Despite his disgust, Gerun was curious. He'd known no one in his family who'd consulted a Jursimmic Priest. The Jursimms were of a faith that existed even before the Religio-College. Ancient. Old. The womb from which *all* the gods on Kanran-9 were said to have been born. *Except* for the god brought by Jon Missionary? "A word?" Gerun repeated. Had the old man really dared the journey into the Labyrinth of Klint? Had he truly paid the fee, participated in the dance, and endangered his soul to the pagans—all for a word?

"And a word we already know, at that," Kalvin said sadly. "'*You'll die because of Christian,*' is what the Priest said, smiling all the while, as if knowing I'd come with the clue already etched in my brain. The Jursimms's face was degenerate from a life of lust and self-indulgence. His stench was so overpowering I almost retched on the spot. 'More!' I demanded. 'I paid the price, and what kind of answer is Christian?' '*You have your answer, tricked from me by your masquerade, I might add!*' the Priest accused me. '*Well, I've kept my bargain, despite your deception. Christian is all the answer I have, all the answer you shall have from me.*'"

Christian. It was not a new word, as Kalvin had said. Even Gerun had heard it often enough before, although it had never been defined. Nor did it have definition now, unless the Priest had known something he wasn't saying. It remained one of the infrequent sounds Jon Missionary had uttered in his lifetime. There were more, equally obtuse and cryptic: Moriah, Aaronic, baptism, sacrament, crucifixion, resurrection. Jon Missionary always got a funny cast to his strange blue eyes—(At the time, blue eyes, except for his, were non-existent on Kanran-9; as soon, Kalvin and Gerun terminated, blue eyes would again be non-existent)—and would speak his strange sounds: Amalek, Zelotes, Philemon, Malachi, Mamre.... All jotted down by those who listened, words to form the litany Gerun had committed to memory, the litany that all Jon Missionary's descendants had at one time committed to memory. Because if the meanings were obscure, even to the brain-damaged man who uttered them, they hinted of wondrous things just beyond the grasp. As if the correct arrangement would form an incantation that would summon forth a whole wealth of secrets to unlock answers to all the unanswered questions. Edom, Edrei, Gennesasret, Egypt, Omer, Ahab.

People? Places? Things? Gibberish from an insane man?

Surely, not gibberish! Because there had been times when the words had been fed back to Jon Missionary, one at a time, or in running sequence, and the sparks of recognition had lit within that man's eyes, and he'd tried to speak more. Tried to speak what?

Nothing Jon Missionary ever said had been translated to anyone's satisfaction. His was a language—yes, it *did* have the insinuated structure and intonation and cadence of a language—but it was no language anyone on Kanran-9 had ever heard, or ever came to understand.

It would have helped, of course, if that man could have learned Kanranian, but it somehow stayed beyond his capacity. Maybe if he'd come to them whole, he could have grasped its intricacies, but the Mysons had gotten to him first, though they swore the *real* damage had been done him by the Xeons. There were no Xeons handy to verify at the time. Even in the present, they appeared only infrequently and then only to exchange goods, as they'd exchanged Jon Missionary, for the much-desired suji-juice. The Xeons, it was said, would sell their mothers (and often did) for suji-juice. Thus, the brain-blank (amateurishly mimicked by Warluck's disfiguring mind-erase) was devised by them to insure that those sold forever forgot their sellers.

Jon Missionary had shown symptoms of Xeon brain-blank. On the other hand, he'd remembered his name. And sometimes he would sit back and look as if he were remembering even more. This was a strangeness that confused, because no one

14

ever remembered anything from before a brain-blank. And he would say those wondrous-sounding words that were first recorded by the scribes of Melina-Lu, then by Melina-Lu herself; then by their children; then passed on to their children's children. It was rumored to be set down within the recordo-writs of the Religio-College that *"Melina-Lu did so lust after the body of the half-wit Jon Missionary that she did intercede with her father, Maxlima II, on the idiot's behalf."* Saving Jon from the same fate (with the exception, it would now seem, of one lone fragment) of his heretical *Book*.

Gerun had never seen the live Jon Missionary, only visual-plays of him. Likewise, neither had Kalvin seen him. But they'd heard the stories passed down from generation to generation. They'd heard, repeated, and memorized his magical words. They'd sensed the specialness of him coursing through their veins.

All these years later, the descendants of Jon Missionary and the Princess Melina-Lu, Kalvin and young Gerun now the last of them, had been marked for death, because of a *Book* fragment none of them had ever seen.

The *Book* had come with Jon through the brain-blank of the Xeons and through his slavery beneath the oppressive yoke of the Mysons. Both Xeons and Mysons were firm respecters of personal talismans and amulets. Had they seen the *Book* as the man's personal talisman? If so, Panrun-Ru had seen it as something more threatening, knowing, as he had, more of books than either the Xeons or Mysons combined. The soldiers who'd captured Jon, during an "unofficial" raid on a Mysons's encampment,

15

had forwarded the stranger and his *Book* to the Religio-College for interrogation. Where Panrun-Ru had ordered the *Book* incinerated as a work of heresy. Only to disobey his own directive and save a fragment. A fragment to surface all of these terns later and spark such terror in the heart of Warluck that he'd systematically set about killing off whatever traces of Jon Missionary had been salvaged, within the gene bank of that man's descendants, by the meddling of a lusting princess.

And who or what was Christian?

CHAPTER TWO

"Had the choice been mine, I would have incinerated the man *before* the book. Preferably incinerated them both.

"It would have forced a power play, my dear Maulaus. One we could ill afford, I might add, after Geulin was named co-conspirator in the assassination attempt. Maxlima II is not alone in thinking more in the Religio College than Geulin had fingers in that dirty pie."

"Still—"

"Besides, the man is a half-wit, obviously a victim of the Xeon brain-blank."

"A brain-blank victim who remembers his name?"

"Who's to say Jon Missionary *is* his real name? Who's to say his other babblings make sense, even to himself?"

"And *if* he remembers?"

"Perhaps we should cross that bridge when we come to it. Until then, the book is out of the way, isn't it?"

—Recording 6-2-4IV.
Conversation between
Panrun-Ru and Maulaus Kif.

GERUN, THE HERETIC, BY WILLIAM MALTESE

Date: 6-04-3-2.
Time: 6:6:6.
Security Clearance:
For No One's Eyes but Mine!

THEY'D BOTH BEEN STARTLED by the whir of the seg-unit, paranoid as they were by the organization out to squash them.

"Obviously not a ferret for us, *this time*," Kalvin said, relief in his voice, "or, we would have been earmarked. There was no broadcast sounded."

"No," Gerun agreed. "Another poor foxlic's hound. The one on us, for the minute, hunting elsewhere."

"Well," Kalvin said with a loud intake of breath, "nothing like a false alarm to hint we may have lingered overly long. I did feel, though, it was important you be made aware of our dire situation. I've felt the noose tightening as of late, and I wondered if there'd be much other opportunity to get to you."

"My thanks, grandfather."

"It would be nice if one of us survived, wouldn't it?" Kalvin said. "The one of us young enough to multiply and pass on the gene bank Jon Missionary gave us."

"You're not too old," Gerun insisted, wondering just *how* old Kalvin really was. Not old enough to remember Jon Missionary, but many terns beyond Gerun's present count.

"Children are of better issue when spawned from the young," Kalvin said. "Remember that whenever you start to get careless. If we're lucky, my children and yours will both arise to greet beneath the moons at Chisan-Time. If not...." He shrugged.

"So, then—" Gerun felt very sad; their parting didn't bode any quick reunions, even if they and their issue *did* survive. "—we part as relatives, *We of the Missionary*, friends, *Meeters at the Future Bend*. Yes?"

"Be healthy, Gerun Missionary," Kalvin said, pulling the boy to him. "Be safe. Be alive. Be fruitful." He kissed Gerun lightly on the forehead, the boy noting the sparkle of tears in the old man's pale blue eyes.

"Where will *you* go?" Gerun asked. Likewise, he was asking where he, himself, would go. Certainly not back to the City where they could more easily tap him. Now, out of their sensor perception, he was better staying put.

"Best you not know my plans or my whereabouts," Kalvin said. "Warluck is clever. Fiss poisoning is uncanny in its distortion of the mentat as it destroys it."

Making mind-reads possible. Making tracers possible. This meant Kalvin would be endangered if Gerun knew and was the first of them caught. Likewise, it was obvious that Kalvin had no desire to know Gerun's plans—what plans? The two were safer, separated. The Missionary gene bank was safer, separated.

"Go with God!" Gerun told him.

"Share the ritual before we part?" Kalvin asked. "Although I've sampled the Jursimms's corruption which makes me less than pure."

"It would be my pleasure to share the ritual, grandfather," Gerun said.

The two dropped to their knees in the darkness, tenting their hands beneath their chins and shutting their eyes. It was a mimicking of Jon Missionary passed down from generation to generation, its meaning unknown. Except it had a magical way of calming a speeding heart, of draining apprehension, of soothing a wearied mind. When Jon Missionary had once been asked why he did it, he'd surprised by saying something almost equivalent to the Kanranian word for *god*. So, his descendants looked upon the ritual as a meeting of god and man on a common plain. Although a meeting with *which* of the many Kanran-9 gods, no one really knew. For Jon Missionary had never been that specific. In fact, if there hadn't been a resulting feeling of "religiousness" found to emanate from the simple ritual, Jon's utterance might long ago have been cast aside as one more haphazard word with no relevance to the original question.

Gerun felt the immediate sense of peace the ritual brought with it, especially when shared with another who was as aware of its magic. As he'd often done in the past, he wondered which of the Kanran-9 deities—if any—had come to Jon Missionary and presented him with this particular mode of silent contact. Jursimms, *The Fulfillers?* No, this was too tame for the rumored rituals of the Labyrinth. Kalvin would have known if this god, in residence, was the same called upon by Jursimmic Priests. Was it Wan Wan-See, *The Sick,* whose shudders could shake the ground and whose pustules could squirt acid to eat the unlucky? Or Zinlac, Xisl, Persif? Or Jab, Jal, Los? Or, was it none of those? Was it a god once known to Jon Missionary and the *Book*, and then known to Panrun-Ru who thought to destroy the god with the pages, incinerating both? A god revealed to Warluck in the book fragment saved? Was that why the Religio-College whispered *heresy* in the same breath they whispered *purge*?

21

"Yes, He has forgiven me," Kalvin said with a sigh, his voice a mere whisper into the silence.

"Who?" Gerun asked, young and wanting all the answers. If Kalvin didn't have them all, it was obvious the old man had more of them than Gerun did.

"Didn't you feel His presence?" Kalvin asked. "Here with us. Called by the ritual."

"Who?" Gerun repeated. He wanted a name.

"Who indeed!" Kalvin replied, getting to his feet and brushing gravel balls from the leatahrer swathing his knees. "Would the incinerated *Book* have told us? Would Panrun-Ru have told us? Could Warluck tell us even now? The god *is* there, whoever He might be. Someone, something, powerful enough to set the Religio-College trembling."

"But not nearly strong enough to save us," Gerun said; more a statement than a question.

"Ah, my boy!" Kalvin said, helping Gerun to his feet. "You resent the prospect of dying only because you are so young."

"And you don't resent it?" Gerun challenged.

"Of course, of course," Kalvin admitted. "But I'm closer to death by natural causes than you are, brought there not by Warluck and his machinations but by the mere passing of time. We all die. If not today, then tomorrow. If not tomorrow, then some other time. If not from fiss poisoning, then from a dew dart shot by a gimlian sprouted unaware in the darkness as we trip on it. Hundreds, thousands, millions of ways to die.

"Yet, Warluck thrives! Protected from death by his gods, while the god of Jon Missionary deserts that man's kin."

"If there *is* a god of Jon Missionary," Kalvin reminded.

"But you insinuated...."

Kalvin raised his hand in interruption. "We must be very careful that we don't read into this more than there is to be read," he warned. "What was Jon Missionary, anyway, but a man without all his faculties? Maybe he wasn't mumbling of God but pretty sounds to entertain his tortured mind, and *we*—Melina-Lu, Panrun-Ru, you, me, Warluck—all misinterpret it wrongly. What then?

"Do you believe he was nothing more or less than an imbecile?" Gerun challenged. It confused him the way Kalvin could go from Jursimmic ritual to Missionary ritual, from belief in Jon Missionary's god, to a denial of Him.

"It's of little importance—*except to me*—what *I* believe is it?" Kalvin answered. "What's important *to you* is what *you* believe. And I would suggest, at the moment, that you're more apt to label Jon Missionary a half-wit than I am."

Gerun flushed with anger and embarrassment, furious that the old man had so easily accessed his mentat, while Kalvin's mentat blocked Gerun's entrance like a wall of grinlind against tansic barbs.

"If He's there, He would help us, is how you reason it," Kalvin said, his voice offering no argument.

"Wouldn't He?" Gerun insisted.

"How am I to say?" Kalvin asked with a voice sounding more and more tired. "How very little we know of Him, Gerun. If, in fact, He is even there. Our link between Him and us was a deranged one. Perhaps all we need to rally His support is the right

23

password, the right key, the proper format for making our request. Every god in the Religio-College has its own format for conversing with humans, doesn't it? Why not this one?"

"But this god should know his linkage to us was faulty, shouldn't He?" Gerun persisted.

"And maybe He knows it wasn't faulty at all," Kalvin argued, playing Delvin's-Advocate. "Maybe we *perceive* it as faulty only because we are too stupid to follow whatever directions have been correctly given."

"You're talking in circles!" Gerun accused.

"I talk as a man who was a gyrolist in his lifetime, not a thelogan," Kalvin reminded. "I know plants, not gods. I can only wish *you* better luck. There's yet time for you to figure out the clues and unravel the puzzles. Granted, not as much time as you might have liked, but...."

He shrugged again, finally looking very much the very old man he was.

"Here, sit with me a minute more," he said, moving to a rough nature-hewn stone and leaning, rather than sitting, against it. He patted a place on the white-veined surface beside him. Gerun joined him.

"There was a plague before you were born," Kalvin said.

"The Bendu Plague," Gerun confirmed.

"In which millions of people died," Kalvin said. "The Religio-College soothsayers pegged the culprit right off. Sillona-Xi, angry because She'd been short-changed the year before when the drought at Kistol made for a poor harvest."

"I don't worship Sillona-Xi!" Gerun snapped.

24

GERUN, THE HERETIC, BY WILLIAM MALTESE

Kalvin breathed his long sign and tried again.

"There was a landslide in the Bytamax Province of Rhinic many terns ago. Six thousand people dead as a result. Three thousand injured. A mountain leveled, three valleys filled to the brim. Why? Because Raglistim was angered by the slowness with which workers were clearing His grotto at Hypernum."

"I don't worship Raglistin!" Gerun informed, angry because he *was* finally getting the point.

"Yes," Kalvin agreed, his mentat having accepted the admission the boy was unprepared to make verbally. "The gods are often as vengeful as they are merciful. Who's to say Jon Missionary's god is any the less vengeful? He did, after all, allow His prophet to endure Xeon brain-blank, didn't He? Not a very pleasant occurrence for any man, from what I've heard. Although it's more merciful to the outer shell than Warluck's sloppier-devised mind-erase."

"But his memory wasn't completely gone," Gerun insisted, referring to Jon Missionary's remembrance of his name and melodious words.

"So, we have always wanted to believe," Kalvin said. "Why? Because it's far more flattering to our egos to think that we've descended from a prophet than from a half-wit, isn't it, my boy?"

If looks could kill, Kalvin would have been a dead man. He knew Gerun, though, and he loved him more than he'd loved any of his other grandchildren. It had always been the boy's passions which had excited Kalvin, which excited him now.

"Which of the Religio-College's pantheon of gods *do* you believe in, Gerun?" Kalvin asked, knowing the answer.

25

"I believe in no god!" Gerun said too quickly, too loudly.

"So easily you deny Him with one breath while expecting Him to succor you with the breath just preceding."

"I meant, I don't know His name," Gerun corrected, feeling like a fool. The old man had led him into the trap like a goosen could lead a flock of gysins to slaughter. Gerun was prepared to admit no more.

"A nameless God, then?" Kalvin persisted. "One not of the Religio-College perhaps?"

Gerun could hide nothing from the old man. The mentat-linkage Kalvin shared with his grandchild was so strong that each feared what loss he would suffer if and when the other died.

"Jon Missionary's god?" Kalvin prodded. Gerun was helpless to keep the answer from him. "I *do* believe in Jon Missionary's god," Kalvin admitted, marveling at the surprise in Gerun's eyes. Did the boy really not know that, really not see that? Did Gerun really believe himself alone in suspecting Jon Missionary was a true messenger from on high? Did Gerun really believe he was the only one angry because the holy message and messenger had gotten so unbearably scrambled along the way?

"Listen to me, Gerun, for I have yet something more to say," Kalvin said, "and we've already dangerously overextended our time in which to say it. It's important that you learn to put Jon Missionary and his legacy in proper perspective, even though it will probably be as impossible for you to manage as it has been for me to do so, not to mention all of the others who have come before us as members of our clan. Will you listen?"

Gerun didn't have to say, yes. His acceptance was conveyed via mentat.

"Only Jon Missionary knows—or once knew—if his arrival was as a messenger from his god, the message hopelessly garbled en route. Jon Missionary is dead. All Melina-Lu's attempts failed that were made to reverse his brain-blank. And there were many attempts at reversal. Remember, too, that Melina-Lu *was* the first true believer. Would a woman merely interested in the physical perfection of a man be so anxious to record that man's every word? On the other hand, maybe she needed something to rationalize the insatiable passion she, a princess of the royal blood, felt for a man who came to her damaged and with a slave brand marring his otherwise perfect body."

"Why must you always take both sides?" Gerun criticized.

"Because I have seen both sides and still made my choice on the side of God," Kalvin explained patiently. Really, Gerun *was* such a child. Was it too much to hope he would survive the careful planning of a skillful exterminator like Warluck? "*You* must see both sides," Kalvin continued.

"Why?" Gerun asked helplessly, ashamed when his mentat, for one brief instant, penetrated through Kalvin's defenses and read there just how much of a child Kalvin really thought Gerun was.

"Why?" Kalvin echoed, his defenses back up. The boy must act like a man. It did Gerun no good at all to see that others—his grandfather included—saw him as a mere boy. Kalvin cursed his slip that had allowed Gerun time to glimpse Kalvin's true feelings. "Because from the moment I leave you, and that shall be soon, I shall be too busy saving myself to save you. You will be on your own. Alone. Warluck, the Religio-College, and all the considerable power that combination can bring against you: your enemy. Where will you be if you don't have at least one god to whom to pray? Not a willowy phantom of a god that may or may not be there, either. What kind of help to you could *that* kind of god possibly be?

"Melina-Lu planted the suspicion of Jon Missionary's god in all of us," Kalvin hurried on. "Flattered by the idea that we were the chosen people, seeing what others hadn't seen, we grew powerful, rich and secure. We became prideful and arrogant. We made enemies and antagonized old ones among the Religio-College. The College was kept at bay, by the way, more because of our connection to the royal house than by any of them truly believing our god could outsmart any of theirs. We grew careless, failing to see that what weakened the Religio-College in Jon Missionary's time was its assumed involvement in an assassination attempt on the life of Maxlima II—and *that* assassination, my young man, was what saved Jon Missionary from the incinerator, *not* the lusting of a princess desirous of taking him to her bed. If Jon Missionary arrived today, he would be incinerated along with his *Book*, because Warluck is far more powerful than Panrun-Ru ever thought of being, and Ruellin VI is far weaker than Maxlima II."

Kalvin's long discourse had left him breathless and panting. Yet, he still had more to say, even through the pale cinolinis on the horizon hinted of the day's first sunrise. "You need faith to survive your upcoming trials, Gerun," Kalvin said. "Faith in God. If the god we've all worshipped in secret all of this time isn't a real enough god for you, marred by your suspicions that He's no more than a madman's ramblings, a lusting woman's rationalizations, an arrogant clan's excuse for feeling better than their friends and neighbors, then cast Him out of your life and believe in Sillona-Xi, or Raglistim, or Gryphis, even in Jursimms. But do believe in *some* god, or you'll die on your own. And that can be a pretty lonely business."

"Warluck must fear our god if he's so intent upon killing Him by killing us," Gerun said.

"Who can truly know Warluck's motivations but Warluck?" Kalvin argued. "They may have nothing to do with God. They may have everything to do with power and/or politics. Ruellin VI is a weak ruler. You and I both know it. By killing us in some holy vendetta, Warluck erodes Ruellin VI's authority even farther by implicating the ruler's Melina-Lu connection in heresy. Save yourself and, then, indulge in ponderings as to why the killer so urgently prowled your doorstep."

Yes, I will save myself, Gerun promised himself. *I'll save me, and I'll save Jon Missionary's god with me. For what kind of god would He be with no worshipers?*

"He found us, didn't He?" Kalvin reminded, having once again read Gerun's mentat. "And look how easily we were won over with just the merest suspicion of His existence. Don't think He'll need you or me when and if He should decide to win new

29

converts. You, on the other hand, need Him to survive. Forget all the Missionary-clan arrogance and
pride piled up over all of this time. We've been
dropped so low that we're liable never to crawl up
out of this hole again. He's not going to help you if
you attempt blackmailing Him into giving you a
helping hand."

Gerun scanned the horizon, cinolinis-to-blinish
hues signaling the increasing nearness of first-day.

"We mustn't be out during the day," Gerun
warned. "We can both hole up here until another
nightfall."

"And wouldn't Warluck just love to stumble
upon the last two eggs in the same basket!" Kalvin
said, his voice resuming its confidence, his body
thrusting off the accumulation of age which had so
stooped it just an instant ago. "We must be together
only in God, until the safety of the Missionary gene
bank is once again secure without us. Until then…"

He took his grandson in one final embrace, his
arms strong, his muscles—another legacy passed
down to all Missionary men from Jon Missionary—
hard against the hardness of Gerun's youthful body.

"Go with God, grandson," he said. Then, he was
gone, slipped into the night so silently that Gerun's
mentat couldn't pick up a trace of it or know the direction the old man had taken.

Gerun dropped to his knees, tented his hands
beneath his chin, and shut his eyes. He prayed to his
god, to Jon Missionary's god, to Kalvin Missionary's god, hoping—deep down in his heart of
hearts—that he wasn't asking help from a deity
whom wasn't there and, what's more, never had
been.

CHAPTER THREE

Carbun 0.00%; Dioxil 0.00%; Oxyfo 0.00%; Morul 0.00%; Defex Morox 0.00%; Sastic Fibrin 0.00%; Hydrul 0.00%....

—Excerpt from the chemo analysis
of binding and pages of the book
confiscated from the man, Jon Missionary.

GERUN KNEW PROPER PROCEDURE. It was dangerous for either Kalvin or him to be up and about during the daylight hours. If Warluck was scouting the Gran Sea for Gerun, that didn't mean he wasn't looking elsewhere as well. Especially since Warluck would be smart enough to suspect Gerun's deception when the servo-ten units hadn't come up with any sign of the young man by now.

On the other hand, unless Kalvin had holed up somewhere very close by, *he* was moving by daylight. And if Kalvin were located by Warluck and interrogated as a result, Gerun's position could be learned from the old man's mentat. However, Gerun was confident that if that worst scenario came to past, his grandfather would hold out long enough to give Gerun warning and a good start after new nightfall.

Gerun burrowed into a fissure in the rock, attempted mentat-rest-cycle and failed. The more he tried, the more difficult it became for him to clear his mind and hibernate for the day. He was too keyed up to relax, filled with surges of conflicting emotions that ran from stark fear, on the one hand, to euphoric exhilaration, on the other. If he was alone, for all intents and purposes, there was a rush he experienced as his entire system geared for the survival ahead.

On the horizon, Kynol-II swung into visibility around Kynol-I. Kanran-9 experienced its second sunrise as brighter light sped into a quickly moving sheet to override the weaker sunbath delivered by Kynol-II's predecessor. The light was accompanied by its own blast of heat that singed the sensitive blossoms of the genu-riff and sent nocturnal-dawn creatures scampering back to subterranean rest holes until twilight.

Gerun sipped sustenance-enforced liquid from the jan-lic container he'd carried with him from the City. He hadn't made his exit from his apartment without being prepared for the eventuality that he wouldn't be returning soon to it. Besides the nourishment in his jan-lic container, he'd brought nutrobars, enero-pills, and three nutri-depressants in case he had to hold off a long time without *any* food or water. He had his C-gun, a couple of ziv grenades, and a goff-gas canister fastened on his belt. He wouldn't be able to hold off any army but, if anything less tried to take him, he'd put up a good show in dying.

He tried again for mentat-rest-cycle, succeeding partially, if still not entirely. Simultaneously, he scanned mentat-wave-lengths for any indication that there had been interference with Kalvin's sending lines and channels. While the old man would have sense enough not to attempt a direct contact if captured, he would surely release a general all-point disturbance pattern that even a less-adept like Gerun would pick up. Especially since Gerun and Kalvin had always been mentat-sensitive.

Heat penetrated Gerun's burrow, and he consciously programmed for lesser neuro-physical functioning. He needed to sweat to maintain a normal body temperature, but the less fluid he surrendered, the better off he was going to be as far as subsistence.

He drifted, all the while leaving enough of his consciousness in charge so that he wouldn't be

33

caught by the enemy unaware. Gerun Missionary had no intention of exiting living with less than a mighty bang. Too many of the Missionary clan had passed into the void without a whimper of protest. If they'd not known that they were the victims of a purge, Gerun was no longer as ignorant. No one was going to expose *him* to fiss poisoning and try to convince *him* it was rare tempmentum—as in the case of his parents—or, Klyrinstok Disease—as in the case of Bet Missionary.

Several times, there was the distant whir of a passing seg-unit, but never a squeal of broadcast being sounded. That verified the seg-units were concerned with other than the location of Gerun Missionary, or they'd spotted nothing to insinuate his presence in the area.

Once, he was wrenched to the brink of consciousness by the more ominous presence of a servo-ten unit but it, too, passed without pause or swerve for closer observation of sunbathed landscape.

In point of fact, the edge of the escarpment, in the combined heat of a full dual day was probably the last place anyone would expect a fugitive to be. Was that why Kalvin had chosen the spot, despite its vulnerability to Cylic blazers and Mylon-probes? Certainly, no one in his right mind would be out in the two suns on a terrain that was as bleak and lifeless as this one. It would have been more logical that a fleeing Gerun would have stuck to exit lanes at least promising the bare essentials for sustaining his existence. The edge of the escarpment offered none of that. However, it was for that very reason that Gerun wouldn't be able to stay there indefinitely. He would need far more life support than he'd carried with him. His main advantage in delay—hopefully—was that Warluck's searchers would be spread out, expecting him to be somewhere ahead of them, rather than following from behind. Not that Gerun wouldn't find himself in particular danger when the enemy turned to their rear and, seeing him, called in reinforcements from *his* rear. The resulting squeeze, he in between, wasn't a moment toward which he looked forward.

The suns rose higher and hotter, the larger chasing the smaller across the dome of clearic sky. Gerun forced himself into a deeper mentat-state. It became easier for him to escape the reality as he reassured himself that he wasn't dead yet and would give Warluck a run for his money. If he'd relied upon Kalvin's protection up until now, the old man had been right in his assessment that Gerun had some in-built survival impulses of his own. Gerun had survived as one of the last two, hadn't he? Over twenty Missionaries had died recently, but here *he* was. That he and Kalvin were the last of their line, the sole containers of Jon Missionary's gene bank, gave Gerun a prime incentive for survival. The same format that had a caused Warluck to so fear the clan Missionary would, now, give Gerun that added push to endure at all cost.

Bockwins hawked their disgusting sounds to the sunshine, the heat of the dual day having forced even those dark scavengers from the sky-lanes. The whole landscape was a blister drained and scabbing; every living thing—Gerun included—had burrowed for safety.

Gerun's inner clock began its audible ticking, tugging him from a complete mentat-rest-cycle. As he counted toward full consciousness, he once again sent a starburst of mentat-waves through the surrounding space, searching out a disturbance he might somehow have missed. Echoes returned with no suspicion of tampering or contact with aggravation, and he breathed a sigh of relief amid hope that Kalvin had eluded and made it to a spot of safety.

The count completed, Gerun resisted, one moment longer, his return to complete consciousness. Once mentat-rest was discarded, he'd be back facing the reality of a world turned against him. He'd be faced with making decisions, any of which could be the wrong one. If he had the advantage of youth and the extra stamina that gave him, he would have traded terns for a bit more of the mentat-expertise Kalvin had carried away with him. It would be mentat, as well as brawn, needed to survive the upcoming ordeal. If Gerun was confident of his brawn—his body rivaling the perfection of Jon Missionary whose physique had set a princess's heart aflame—he self-admittedly wasn't the brightest the Missionary clan had produced in the mentat department. Not that he was stupid. He was a recognized expert at deciphering Fin-rick codes, unraveling them faster than most: a talent that insinuated he had mentat-talents somehow trapped inside and kept hidden despite many a tutor's attempts to dislodge them. So good had he been at the Fin-rick-code games, he'd once had thoughts of attempting to decipher Jon Missionary's gibberish, once and for all, but he'd never plunged forward with any real enthusiasm. Not only because he didn't feel himself up to it—

and he *didn't* ever feel up to it—but Kalvin had been right in that it was always more satisfying to the ego to believe one descended from a prophet than from a blithering idiot. Decoding Jon Missionary's words, and finding them nothing but slush, would have denied Gerun the heritage he'd been raised to believe was his—as a Missionary—and no one else's beyond the family clan.

He shook his head to clear it, reminding himself that other clan members, more knowledgeable than he, had tried to decipher the language of Jon Missionary and failed. Was their failure based entirely on the exhaustion of their abilities or on—as with Gerun—their inability to cope with the truth of less-than-admirable beginnings?

He emerged from mentat-rest-cycle, possessed of the belief that it really no longer mattered from whom or from what he'd descended. He was alive, no matter what the cause, and the thing was to stay that way. If he survived, it would be proof enough that he came with a gene mix superior enough to outwit the likes of Warluck and the whole Religio-College.

His eyes opened to darkness. He read his wrist-indicator, pleased that his inner clock and the mechanical one had ticked in unison. He had more than enough incentive to get things right, a reassuring thought for someone who'd—before now—been unable to muster the willpower to master mentat as well as he might have.

He stretched, consciously commanding muscle groups to respond to the stretching and limber beneath it. If mentat-rest had a marvelous way of leaving a body supple, Gerun could afford no chances of straining at this stage of the game. His mind and body had to be perfectly one, without flaw, if he was going to save himself to see a new day.

He released his claim on the burrow, emerging beneath night sky hardly lightened by the dull-almost-invisible circle of Moon Myl on the edge of the horizon. Moon B was higher yet, darker yet, its outline a barely discernable crescent of black against blackness.

Gerun listened, honing natural devices which would have to hold him in good stead against the competition of mechanical marvels Warluck would have sent out to fetch him. He heard the *pop* of a siston pod exploding somewhere near, extending tentacles to night air. He heard a loonal's soft and breathless cry. A tander moth died in the glue of a jinjax in the distant darkness, fanning the glue's inviting fragrance (which had lured the moth to destruction in the first place) to other potential victims.

Moon Mithric would rise in two hours. It, of Kanran-9's three moons, supplied the most nocturnal light and, thus, the most danger to Gerun who would have preferred no Mithric moonrise. Still, he wouldn't get far if he were forced into traveling only in complete darkness. To get as far as he wanted, as fast as he wanted, he needed his days *and* his nights for movement. The farther he exited the influence of the City, the better off he was going to be.

The City had once provided a protective aura; Warluck lived there, the Religio-College was headquartered there, and the decision had apparently been made to avoid fouling the nest until the very last. So, those of the Missionary clan who'd lived

there, Gerun included, had been saved until last—
except when they'd obliged by going on holiday,
like Gerun's parents, offering the opportunity to
blame something other than an official—or unofficial—purge for their infection. Now, however, the
City was as dangerous to Gerun as the glue of the
jinjax was to the tander moth.

But what of the dangers for him beyond the
City? At least, the City still offered an obscurity
even for a Missionary within the numbers who
populated the massive warrens of apartments, business cubes, foundation giants, eco-units. In his present baggy clothes, the perfection of his body well
hidden, he might still be mistaken for the bulky, but
less delineated Krisan, or the big-boned skeletal
Fleeson. It was only naked, or in form-clinging lex-
tex that Gerun's musculature revealed its true
uniqueness. With his hue-brown lenses (ground over
six terns ago when Gerun had masqueraded as a
brown-eyed Kirisan at the Tan-tan Ball—surprising
by winning third), he might not stand out in any
City crowd. However, in the periphery regions, he
would be a stranger among the lower-numbers-than-
City-population permanents. He would be noted,
categorized. Reported to the local authorit-block?
Checked against unofficial purge lists? Identified?
Arrested? Injected? Dead?

He decided upon a compromise between City
and periphery. A *town*. Granted, no town was the
labyrinth offered by the City, but towns were farther
away from the hub and, thus, less susceptible to the
Religio-College power source at City-Central. The
farther from the City, the less agents on the prowl.

What town, though? If he didn't know, how could Warluck venture a guess? Maybe Dixtown on the Trysal belt. A boom town, that one, filled with all kinds of shady get-quickers who would be as less likely to question as to be questioned. Maybe Jeninstown, there to masquerade as one more vagrant pulled by the job opportunities from irrigation lines being stretched as arteries from the newly completed Grun Dam. Maybe Yextown, where Gerun's strength and muscle would be appreciated in leveling the jungle and setting irritant Bagbuns to the torch. Although, the young man doubted he'd have the stomach for so destroying any life form, even the disgusting, irritant-squirting Bagbuns.

He'd get to his mobile and flash a map on its video. He'd throw a random dance-dot and watch to see where it alighted. What better way to pick his destination? Meanwhile, Warluck would be involved in a complex thought game, trying to decide what mental gymnastics Gerun would utilize and how Warluck might duplicate them. Well, Gerun would fool him and select haphazardly.

He slowed his progress, stopped, and sniffed the air, listened, and synraxed landmarks so he could assure he was nearing his stash area. Having mobiled from the City, he'd not taken the mobile near the rendezvous spot, thinking the mechanics of the thing—if detected—would be a standout on the escarpment edge. However, where he had left it, along a meandering trail of the Xenxic Mound, there were derelict mobiles left abandoned from the time of the Cerean Rusts. One more seemingly inoperable mechanical among those heaps would raise no eyebrows. Unless a suspicious eye probed closer, trying to determine why the mobile had been purposely hidden. And who would bother with that in the face of the surge of timtimolic growth which had tented most of the largest metallic leftovers? Surely, not even Warluck's henchmen, suspecting Gerun's mobile among the offered sound-echoes, would have the patience to probe personally every timtimolic tent.

Mithric Moon had just poked its sapphiric luminescence above the line of horizon, flushing pale blue into the darkness, when Gerun stopped again. The boulders around him sprouted lun-lichen that made the stone darker than the fading darkness. Fansheans grew profuse from every crack. Tapgrass rose to his thighs, making whishing sounds against his floppy cloak as he walked. The whishing might have been detected by a servo-ten unit, computed as human-not-inhuman motivated, but it was a risk Gerun had decided to take. Avoiding the tapgrass would have meant avoiding the flat pathways. Besides, jumping from boulder to boulder would have caused detectable sounds of its own. This way was faster.

Gerun divined no sign of Kalvin. Not that the old man had passed this way—coming or going—but if he had, he'd been clever in covering his tracks. Of course, Gerun wasn't a servo-ten unit, but he would have bet a Tilinian cube that even a servo-ten wouldn't have computed Kalvin's passage by the evidence offered.

Mithric Moon propped higher, and Gerun was thankful for umbrella Fansheans that kept him in shadow. If his calculations were right, it wasn't all that much farther.

He dropped at the sound, his whole body in tap-grass, his nose smelling the fragrance of the bruised blades and stems he'd trampled. Normally, the stenchy smell wouldn't have risen above his waist, and he wasn't pleased he'd joined it below. But, there *had* been a sound. A light, too.

Get your act together, Gerun, he mentated, consciously regulating his pulse and breathing to more normal levels. *Replay the trigger stimuli.* A sound. Of boot against rock. *A light.* Of a wicken-lighter, one of the new kind that flamed similan and kept cigars burning that color to their stubs.

From where the origins? Up and to his right. High up. On the pyramidal summit of piled boulders.

He rolled to his back, attempting to ignore the additional stenchy of disturbed tap-grass.

Yes, he saw them up there. Two of them, silhouetted with a mobile. A polici-sci mobile, blue and green. A periphery patrol. Farther from the City than normal. Looking for him?

They were way too noisy to be contemplating an ambush. The one actually laughed. Female. The other's voice was low and muted. Another laugh. Another flash of similan as the wicken-lighter flared again. Gerun's imagination, or was there really another smell above that of tap-grass? A heavy smell that didn't rise with the wind but sank to ground level and spilled down the rock face like molasses. Marlina? If so, the polici-sci in the mobile were some big-spenders. Marlina cost big cubes, even on the black-market—when it could be had. The Jursimms held a monopoly on the weed. Independent growers, if ferreted, were hauled off to Winshora Camp for hard labor.

Another mobile! Landing lights on. The sweep of tan-green shining over Gerun on the tap-grass. Thank God, it wasn't a find. A find would have had him for sure, isolated him, and kept him pinned.

He was sweating. Beads of perspiration bathed his forehead, cheeks, chin, neck, chest, stomach, and crotch. What a waste of moisture!

"Careful!" someone shouted from the pyramidal pile. Sounding angry but accompanied by Marlina-high-pitched laughter. The landing mobile teetered precariously on the edge, and then set down on firmer ground out of Gerun's focus.

"I brought Tarra to the party!" announced someone a few moments later. "Tarra, you know Grego and Sula."

"Tell the whole Jursimms-filled world, why don't you?" an angry voice retorted amid more high-pitched giggles.

"Sorry." The apology was carried within the Marlina fumes that drooled the mountain to Gerun within the tap-grass on the pathway below.

The combination of tap-grass stenchy and burned Marlina weed made Gerun nauseous, giving him no more desire to smoke than ever. He'd been tempted only once, present when Cousin Ted once lit up. Cousin Ted, dead of fiss-poisoning-mas-querading-as-kinchin's-syndrome. Which fiss vari-ant had Warluck approved for that? Fiss-two? In Marlina? Anyway, Ted's mother had caught them, pulled them to the visual screen, and played back the tape on Sanson Missionary. Before: an attractive young man, blond hair, blue eyes, athletic build. After: an unattractive middle-aged man, thinning hair, watery blue eyes, grotesquely fat body. Sanson Missionary: black sheep, disappointment to his mother and father, indulger at Marlina smoke parties, drinker at winber-barrel parties, and violator of *The Prime Example*. Dead at thirty-six. "There's where you're both headed!" had proclaimed Ted's mother, scaring Gerun (but not her son) into a life-without-weed.

Jon Missionary had been The Prime Example that all clan members had been expected to emulate. The Prime Example that neither Sanson nor Ted had followed. Before Jon Missionary had died, he'd sorted through a whole gamut of Kanran-9 eats and drinks, discarding Marlina, winber, kraxlin, steaming teafee, and several others, refusing to imbibe. The longer he lived, compared to the eaters of kraxlin, the drinkers of steaming teafee and winber, the smokers of Marlina, the easier it became to suspect the merits of Jon Missionary's example. Though little good it had done Ted, dead at sixteen from fiss-poison-induced-kinchin's-syndrone, but it might yet help Gerun live long enough to escape Warluck and pass on Jon Missionary's gene bank to a new batch of children.

How long a time passed before Gerun convinced himself he wasn't the hunted but the uninvited-at-a-Marlina-party? He didn't know how long. He did know that, accident or not, there were mechanics in those two mobiles to ferret him out of hiding. Aware of the telltale smells of Marlina, not wanting it to attract unwanted guests, might not the polici-sci scan to be sure the area was clear? Maybe it was already being done, right then.

And this was the luck brought him by Jon Missionary's god? Gerun would probably be better to place his faith in Jursimms, under the circumstances. After all, Marlina was Jursimms' sacred weed.

However, no god was liable to offer support to someone who couldn't help himself, and Gerun hadn't exhausted his options yet. He was wasting time by waiting for them to scan, waiting for them to find him. As if he really didn't believe he had a chance of a nowball in ledheat of outmaneuvering Warluck. Well, he *did* have a chance!

He rolled to his belly and erected only as far as a low crouch. He moved bent low so he still smelled bruised tap-grass mingled with the headier aroma of burnt weed. He made more noise than he should, anxious to clear the area before the scope of the polici-sci scans. All the while, he anticipated the isolating find glaring suddenly on his progress. Making the polici-sci curious? Or, making them only laugh high-pitch louder at having flushed a potential joiner from cover? Would they interrupt their fun and games for harassment? Did Marlina mellow, slow reaction time, and dull the senses? Weren't those the reasons Jon Missionary had excluded it from clan usage? Who could know? Jon Missionary had babbled, and Melina-Lu had interpreted babble as *she* saw fit. Her children and her children's children had interpreted as *they* saw fit. Until a weed Jon Missionary had possibly discarded on a mere whim had inadvertently passed into Missionary-clan gospel as a no-no.

Gerun counted his steps, estimated distances assumed scan-span possible by the mechanics of the polici-sci mobile units. If he could just make it a little farther without detection. If he could just round this next bend. There! Ah, yes! Except, maybe, he'd not calculated correctly. He'd never been all that good at mathmag. He *could* have been wrong. Safer up the path a bit, through here, around here. Looking back over his shoulder, no sign of them. He was surely safe here.

So, where *was* he? He'd been so interested in getting away that it had slipped his mind where he was supposed to be escaping *to*. He'd not reach any town on foot. He needed his mobile. Which he'd parked and concealed where?

A mentat-pause. A moment for calm reflection. Take it easy. Take it very easy. Don't panic! Think! Analyze. Check for landmarks. The blue-reflected light of Mithric Moon made visibility easy: as much a bonus for him, now, as for his enemy.

There, he recognized that outcropping. And that branching fissure like a twin-headed smo-snak. And that boulder wedged against that cliff face and supporting that gnarled deadness of a Purntic trunk. He only needed to head left. Except left was blocked by an unstable dirt slide. So, he'd keep going straight until he was around the slide. No problem. No problem at all. So, why was his heart pounding? So, why was he running scared? He heard no bray of foxlic-hounds behind him. Did he?

He stopped. He listened. He heard nothing but his own breathing, backed by a wind arising off the barrenness of the distant escarpment. A faint, female high-octave laugh, muted by his physical separation from it, sounded in unthreatening punctuation.

GERUN, THE HERETIC, BY WILLIAM MALTESE

Calm. Calm. Mentat-calm. Except it wasn't working. He couldn't concentrate, couldn't empty his mind, couldn't think of anything beyond the stenchy of fear emanating from his own body and overpowering even the scents of Marlina and bruised tap-grass.

He dropped to his knees, resorting to ritual as a last resort. He tented his hands beneath his chin, shut his eyes, and waited. Actually surprised when the fear inside of him receded to a bearable intensity, even if the ritual didn't dissolve his fear completely.

CHAPTER FOUR

"Some kind of joke, is it? Shall I bring Panrun-Ru in and let him laugh along with us?"

"No joke, believe me. We've run them through twice."

"This means the equipment has gone haywire."

"We ran a recordo-unit cartridge and a libro-card through as controls and got prefect readouts on the both."

"You're not telling me *these* readouts *are accurate!*"

"I'm merely showing you what the equipment is telling us. I don't know what to make of it, and you're next in line on my chain of command."

"Well, *I* say you run them through again."

"And if we receive the same readouts?"

"Then, you call in a mechanic to look at the machines."

"Although controls continue to read perfectly?"

"Something somewhere is malfunctioning. There is simply no way you could feed bonding and pages through and get something like *these* as correct results. You know that; I know that. Agreed?"

"Agreed."

"Then, find the malfunction before Panrun-Ru comes down here and finds it for us!"

GERUN, THE HERETIC, BY WILLIAM MALTESE

—Excerpt from Lab-tech #3.
Recordo unit 6643B.
Tech-Maj Domino Moore and
Tech-Min Wilton Proust.
Date: 6-4-3.
Time 4:3:6.

GERUN ACTIVATED the dance-dot on his mobile video and watched it wander the map segments projected beneath it. When dance-dot stopped, map-freeze resulting, Gerun checked the town nearest the dot.

Mofftown. It rang no bells. He called up an explain on the video panel: *Mofftown, Ceres Province, Krasto Section 6-point-2, Vector coordinates 16-12-reversed. Population: Major-max-minor. Major support: Clarion pools, Morjox source, Seabun manufacture.*

It wasn't an appetizing fare that the haphazard selection had set up for him. He had little desire to meld with the skimmers of Clarion pools, nor to mine Morjox at clabinhation depths, nor to oversee robots punch-plugging Kanran-9's seabun output. He would have stood out like a sore thumb in any of those occu-lines. He'd been hoping for something a little closer to Krisan or Fleeson borderlines. What was the point of being able to pass for Krisan or Fleeson if he wasn't headed for a town or occu-line in which Krisan or Fleeson were employ? The chances of either being in Mofftown were about one in 1,200. In fact, he ran it through the mobile computa just to be sure. He'd been generous. According to mobile computa, the odds were one in 2,146.

He reactivated the dance-dot. This time in-feeding data that was pertinent. Although by doing so, he knew he was eliminating elements of the haphazard. He was setting guidelines and limits that Warluck would be, likewise, feeding into a similar computa elsewhere. *"With brown-hue lenses, the boy could pass for a Krisan or Fleeson,"* Warluck would be saying. *"Highly unlikely he'd be off to Mofftown, wouldn't you say? More likely Tinttown."*

Tinttown exactly where the dance-dot stopped, next time around.

Tinttown, Box Province, Dranco-shish Section, Twelve-point-six, Vector coordinates 212-640. Population: Major-min-minor. Major support: Cryne growth, Cepol harvest, Davin-thee crop.

Plenty of Krisan and Fleeson there. Ideal? *Too* ideal?

Gerun sat back in his mobile, condemning himself for not having more thoroughly gotten his escape plan together before now. He'd stashed the brown-hue lenses, a food supply, even the mobile (used and untraceable), but he'd never pinpointed just where he would go and how he would get there. Always, because he'd assumed there would be some other members of the clan alive, he'd thought to run to family. How quickly that had become impossible. Twenty-two family members wiped out in no time. Two to go. *One* to go if Gerun didn't wise up and use his smarts. There was no way he could spend forever in this mobile, beneath this concealing tent of timtimolic.

Where, he wondered, had Kalvin decided to go? Kalvin wouldn't have been sitting around twirling his thumbs. He would have had a concrete plan, up to and including contacting Gerun. Kalvin would know just exactly where he was headed and how he planned to get there without detection by Warluck or Religio-College henchmen. Why couldn't Gerun be as on top of it all?

GERUN, THE HERETIC, BY WILLIAM MALTESE

He pressed the motor-engage, and the mobile exited timtimolic tent through a neat little hole made by forward pressure. He steered to parallel the lights of the city, having no intentions of intruding that warren until it was safer than it was now with Warluck in residence. There could be no turning toward the escarpment, either. He'd already rejected that route as unsafe, its terrain hardly able to keep Bockwins in enough phlegm for hawking. Besides, he had no desire to get anywhere near the two polici-sci mobiles that had brought their riders to a secluded Marlina party.

He wasn't sure where he was going, but there was a certain satisfaction to being on his way. Maybe if he just played it by ear, Jon Missionary's god would be there to steer the way. Then, again, maybe He wouldn't. Gerun was liable to be in sad straights if he turned his survival over to pure chance. Whether it was mentally and physically beyond his capabilities, he still had to have a plan of his own making. He *had* to decide where he was going. He needed that sense of order in his life. Once he had that, he could drift from it later, amending as the situations warranted.

A servo-ten unit passed across the periphery of his scan-range. He watched its bleep with apprehension, because if he'd mechanically noted it, he could assume the recognition had been mutual. However, that particular servo-ten unit wasn't likely programmed to search for a mobile six-tern old. Gerun, with Tilinian to last, a substantial amount of his savings stuffed in the trunk, would be more apt to be found in a new model. His new model, though, was parked in the basement garage of his apartment.

Warluck would know Gerun and fled in something else. The chances of the boy walking out of the city were paramount to nil.

Traffic bleeps registered on the video, and Gerun fought any impulse to steer clear. If anyone official were monitoring the travel lanes, it would have looked mighty suspicious were a mobile to weave this way and that with seeming attempt to maintain aloneness. More often than not, mobiles were apt to travel in convoys like the one intercepted by Gerun's mobile scan.

The convoy was mainly mobilesems bringing produce from periphery to the City. It crossed Gerun's pathway at a right angle, and he rode through a gap without severing its in-line lock-up.

A single-seater mobile whipped by within visual range and bleeped front-san lights in friendly hello. Gerun signaled back his own friendly greeting but hoped it wasn't a fun-and-gamesman on the other end. Gerun had no desire to attempt explaining why he wasn't "into" the prevailing free-and-easy promiscuity of Kanran-9. Jon Missionary had so pronounced—(rather, Melina-Lu had so interpreted)—that bodies were designed for one-on-one relationships, marital-bound. The everyday man on the street might come to marital bonding with a lifetime of experimental sexual indulgences, but members of the clan Missionary were expected to be far more innocent.

The single-seater left the tracking plain, and Gerun breathed easier. It would have been tempting, in retrospect, had the mobile been a fun-and-gamesman from whom Gerun might sample some of the forbiddens of which he'd been deprived throughout his so-far life. If he'd been on his own before now—for most intents and purposes—after his parents' deaths (except, of course, for the mentat-overlook by his grandfather), he'd still been held in check by thoughts of how the other clan members would react if he were caught in the act of blatantly transgressing. However, who was to know now? Everyone was gone but Gerun and Kalvin. So, he guessed it was Kalvin's continued existence which left him breathing easier when he'd been saved from temptation. Then again, if Jon Missionary was a messenger from God and had really gotten across his message that fun-and-gamesmen were not acceptable companions, then Gerun would have been walking on an even thinner religious edge by surrendering to physical pleasure. He did, after all, believe he received spiritual contentment from the ritual. If that was because there was a god in attendance, then Gerun would just as soon not antagonize Him.

More lights on the scan-screen! A traffic stall? A convey formation? To avoid or not to avoid? Blue-green flash of a polici-sci unit in attendance, but that was to be expected. There was no evidence of an official blockage-barrier impeding the lead mobile. Had there been, Gerun would have been made paranoid by the prospects of an out-and-out search in progress—for him. Granted, as far as he knew, neither Warluck nor the Religio-College had made the purge of clan Missionary official. They'd done very well with things left *un*official, thank-you very much. However, if Kalvin and Gerun had been finally eluded their chasers for too long, the powers that be might well have come out more brazenly to extinguish the last two of the Jon-Missionary residue.

Gerun stalled his mobile behind the one presently at the end of the line. Had he swerved to avoid linkage, how many mobile scanners would have noted and marked his anti-social behavior with suspicion? How many of those would have passed on the tidbit to City-Center? After all, convoys, at this hour of the night, were the thing, weren't they? They were safety measures in a time and age that weren't the safest.

The mobile ahead buzzed Gerun's communicator. Gerun had hoped the driver unfriendly. He had no desire to chitchat, not with the granddaddy computa of the Religio-College waiting in the City for feed-in of visual and speech for analysis.

He fuzzed audio-visual. "Afraid this thing's not working the way it should," he apologized. "Not enough Tilinian in this world or the next to fix this clinker."

"Know what you mean," sympathized the reply. A man's voice. A man not driving a clinker, either. Not the latest model, mind you, but a recent one in damned good shape. His visual leaned a little too heavily toward the gream spectrum but, aside from that, was excellent in comparison to the fuzz-blot Gerun fed him. He had a wife. Gerun was getting her sleeve on the video feed. He had at least one kid, too. Kids, even when unseen, made unmistakable noises. This one was old enough to talk.

"Want do-ru, do-ru, do-ru," the kid was chanting from somewhere just off picture.

"Give David his do-ru, will you, Fanina!" the man insisted.

Gerun smiled a smile that he thought would be sympathetic, but it didn't convey in the fuzzy transfer.

"Where are you headed?" the man asked. His attention was back on Gerun's scrambled image. "Thorntown?"

Thorntown was as good a place as any, but Gerun didn't want to commit to someone's possible hometown when Gerun knew absolutely nothing about it. That could have led to all sorts of complications after a few decimals of conversing on the road. What other town was in the general direction of Thorntown?

"Heading on to Shagtown," Gerun said, pinpointing another border settlement on the computa-map grid.

"Don't envy you *that*," the man consoled.

"Oh?" Gerun responded, simultaneously wondering if he should be acting more concerned by the man's obvious concern.

"That Westicks raid on the Power Cor installation," the man elucidated.

What Westicks raid on what Power Cor installation?

"I heard they'd closed all access," the man added.

Clan Missionary didn't believe in lying but, in this case, a lie seemed better warranted than the truth. "I'm hoping, somehow, to squeeze through."

Here comes the polici-sci unit," the man announced. "Maybe we can get an update."

"No, that's...." Gerun couldn't finish before the man had punched them both into the polici-sci mobile's communication network.

"Where you folks headed?" greeted an officer.

"My family and I are to Thorntown," the man answered. "The mobile behind us is to Shagown. Heard the latest from there?"

"You're headed for Shagtown?" the officer asked Gerun. Computa-readout indicated that he was programming for better reception. He seemed, somehow, to get it, because he obviously recognized Gerun's youth. "Headed back on a City SCH vacation, are you, kid?"

Gerun didn't have the faintest idea about SCH's educational scheduling. He'd always had private tutors. No Missionary, except possibly Jon Missionary (who, after all, knew?) had ever attended public SCH.

"My mother hasn't been feeling well," Gerun said, deciding he was on safer ground going that route.

"He's worried he might not be able to access because of the Westicks raid on the Power Cor installation," the man clarified.

"No one said it was a Westicks raid," the officer countered.

"I heard…." the man began.

"And *I* heard it was merely a regular Class-II power-out," the not-to-be-one-upped officer interrupted. "A clogged peuses connection, or something like that. The Westicks wouldn't dare try anything."

"I'm glad to hear that," the man said. He was obviously someone who knew how to back off. Gerun was sure the guy would live to be a ripe old age. Which was more than Gerun could say for himself.

"I'd check in with the authorit-block as soon as you get to Thorntown, kid," the officer suggested.

"They'll know the scoop. In the meantime, I'm assuming you both want to engage for convoy?"

"Right!" Gerun and the man said in unison. Gerun punched the gyro-mag that would keep him honed in on the forward car until disengage in Thorntown.

"And thanks officer," Gerun said, hoping that would end the conversation. He didn't like the way the red light blinked on his console in indication that the officer continued his effort to achieve a computa-enhanced visual of Gerun.

"Be *sure* to contact the authorit-block in Thorntown," the officer insisted, holding communication for a few moments longer. "And don't go telling them I said access was open if you get there and it isn't. Sometimes we're the last to know what's happening around here." Did that mean there *could* have been a Westicks raid?

"I will, sir," Gerun promised.

"Hold for one further engage!" the officer announced, and Gerun checked the approaching mobile that was speeding up from behind him for convoy-join. It wasn't a welcome sight. Gerun would now be hemmed in at both ends with no chance of sloughing off somewhere en route.

"Holding," Gerun informed, preparing to disconnect the officer and the mobile owner's audio-visuals at one and the same time and prefacing with, "Ridsin-bat is fading. Guess I'll have to preserve for emergencies."

"Right!" the man agreed, but the officer was less understanding.

GERUN, THE HERETIC, BY WILLIAM MALTESE

"You get that ridsin-bat fixed the very next opportunity, kid," the officer instructed. "Being without one is *not* the safest way to drive the periphery."

Gerun disconnected and sat back in his seat. He unwrapped a nutro-bar. He felt the gyro-mag of the mobile behind grab hold for lock-in. Moments later, Gerun's mobile jerked forward and, then, began its movement as part of the convoy.

For better or for worse, he was headed at least as far as Thorntown. And somewhere up the way, if rumor could be believed, the Westicks were already beginning to make use of the munitions purchased at the expense of how many clan Missionary dead? Gerun couldn't wish the Westicks luck. Brewers of fiss poisoning, they were a mysteriously sinister lot who'd supplied the fatal ingredients that allowed Warluck his elimination of Missionaries under a variety of different guises. However, Gerun could wish that the Westicks' kicking up of their heels would cause a diversion to keep Warluck and the Religio-College busy while Kalvin and Gerun slipped through the trap so maliciously being set for them.

CHAPTER FIVE

"It's impossible!"

"So said I before personally checking procedure for accuracy."

"You checked it?"

"And double-checked it. Then, I ordered the book incinerated. For if the container was so heretical, imagine the contents!"

"But what's it mean?"

"You tell me."

"But it's too fantastic!"

"Nonetheless."

"It goes against everything."

"Not info to be spread around, I'm sure you'd agree."

"Who else knows?"

"Maulaus, of course. And the two Lab-techs involved with the analysis. I've already made arrangements to terminate the latter."

—Recording 8-1-1III.
Conversation between Panrun-Ru
and Safroi Martin.
Date: 9-8-6-1. Time: 12:6:3.
Security Clearance: FNOEBM!

THE EXPLOSION BROUGHT GERUN from
mentat-rest-cycle without any accompanying count.
He came to consciousness amid the startling realization that the mobile ahead of him was gone, raining
its pieces in a brightness lighted by detonations
above and to either side of the travel-lane.

The convoy was broken, its linkages torn at several other spots along the line by similar direct hits
like the one that had released Gerun's mobile and
sent it veering. Behind him, the still-following mobile just managed to detach before Gerun's vehicle
toppled over the steep embankment.

Debris from multi-mobiles clattered around Gerun, banging his mobile and denting its surface. His
mobile's face-shield cracked as a particularly large
segment collided with resounding impact that had
Gerun sure he'd be squashed when the missile collapsed the plexi-plast. Luckily, the face-shield held,
the boulder-sized ruin rebounding as the depressed
plexi-plast played sling.

Assassination was what Gerun's mind calculated first. Less clever than Kalvin, Gerun was sure
he had somehow left a trail, and this was the result.
Death of next-to-last Missionary on a convoy-
bound-for-Thorntown. It wasn't exactly the way
he'd planned to go. But if he couldn't be any clev-
erer than this in shaking his pursuers, then what
kind of end-game could he expect *but* this?

More flashes of destruct. A Cylic-blazer phase
weaved the skyline with color, zapping another
three mobiles in the process. A sent-flying-by-blast
mobile hit ground close to Gerun, splattering his
mobile with gravel balls.

GERUN, THE HERETIC, BY WILLIAM MALTESE

It was only the sloppiness of it all that made it seem wrong. This was down-and-out slaughter, using big guns and wiping out innocents in the bargain. At Chinsore, Gerun had been alone in his exposure to the wave. At Ron-ron, he'd been alone when the pellets were launched from the hills. Here, he *wasn't* alone.

In fact, occupants of several mobiles were coming out of this far worse than he was. To verify, a mobile exploded like a starburst, scattering its scraps, human and otherwise, to the atmosphere and landscape.

A Religio-College that thought nothing of massacring innocents was likely to lose as many converts as gain new ones. It wasn't their style. And if they were so intent upon terminating Gerun this way, why had his mobile suffered less damage than it had? Even the first shot, the one which had severed him from the convoy line, hadn't destructed his mobile but the one ahead. Granted, that might have been a faulty shot, but wouldn't' it have been followed by a more accurately aimed barrage once Gerun's mobile was disabled and lying aslant a ditch?"

Not that Gerun *wasn't* in danger. The Cylic blazers were completing weaves that left no one on the receiving path safe for the moment. But Gerun could have been in worse shape had the firers concentrated on him as their chief objective.

So, what then, if not an assassination attempt? Thieves? Maybe if Gerun's mobile had been alone, but thieves attacking a convoy was unheard of since the terns of the Glipsin Band who'd been completely eliminated for overstepping the boundaries of decorum. Had there been another such band in operation, word would have spread to the extent that even Gerun would have known of it. No, it had to be Religio-College goons.

A blaze-laze detected Gerun's dormant mobile and whapped it a good one. The leading third of the vehicle disintegrated in a blossoming of mobile guts. The heat melted a large hole in the already shattered face-shield. Gerun's hair singed in the process.

He ejected, eventually landing with a thud that knocked his breath out of him. A meandering blaze-laze scorching had preceded the arrival of his land-cush, providing smoking ground. Had it occurred only moments later, Gerun would have entered into disintegration, along with minerals, instead of just ending up breath-deflated.

He disengaged from the land-cush and immediately found a shallow burrow in which to nestle, wishing the ground crease were deeper, wishing its width and length smaller. He needed confinement in which to hide, the deeper the better. The less of him exposed, the less of him likely to get dissolved if and when a blaze-laze returned. His only consolation was that blaze-lazes apparently had bigger and better targets to deal with at the moment. Fireworks continued going off on all sides, and the cam-en-block of a destruct mobile collided with the earth in a dirt-splattering erupt that partially buried Gerun. Hot metal pellets from ground and cam-en-block rained down upon and burned him. Hopefully, none were fiss-dipped.

A mentat-thought-analysis would have been in order. Gerun needed in-put and examination to figure out what was happening. However, knowing what was needed to put the occurrences into proper perspective, and having the ability to instigate a mentat-thought-analysis calmly, were two entirely different things. There was no way he could summon the concentration required to mentat-dissect what was happening all around him.

There had been a kid in the mobile in convoy ahead of him. Gerun did know that much. No way had mother, father, *or* child survived the explosion which had brought Gerun awake to the beginnings of this progressing nightmare.

There was, he realized for the first time, the simultaneous retort of fire-backs. Their sounds had probably been there all along, but Gerun hadn't registered them. Obviously, there were mobile drivers far quicker in their reflexes than Gerun was. Gerun hadn't even gotten around to drawing his C-gun. That's how on top of it he was (wasn't).

Not that his C-gun would have probably done all that much damage, especially in the face of his not having even isolated his enemy at the moment.

He should have isolated his enemy!

But what good was a C-gun against Cylic blazers and blaze-laze? He was up against some major firepower, here. Expensive to boot. The *really* big time. Hardly the stuff ordinary thieves were capable of getting their hands on. More likely an army, or....

He drew his C-gun and checked, by feel, to make sure he'd brought ziv grenades and goff-gas canister along on his belt. *Finally,* he was beginning to think like a soldier under fire. He should have nurtured that mentality and reflex a long time ago. It wasn't as if he hadn't known there were people out to kill him. He'd survived three assassination attempts. Easily. Too easily. Counting on his natural dexterity and not his brains to do the trick? Counting on Kalvin somewhere in the wings? Well, he was all by himself this time around. Wherever Kalvin had gotten himself off to, Gerun wasn't feeling any mentat-protect zooming in from near or afar.

He poked his head above ground, sorry he couldn't be more daring, sorry he was so frantically afraid. This was the Religio-College unveiled and not needing to operate within any civilized guise. These were the blazers he'd feared on the escarpment, so why was he so surprised to find them awaiting him here?

A survivor of three assassination attempts, Gerun had never been subjected to the sight of innocents dead, dying, about to die. He'd not smelled their blaze-lazed bodies scenting the air with disaster. This was blatant overkill!

He spotted a fire-back and followed it to point of origin. Once again, someone was more a natural at battle conditions than Gerun. The firer of the Phase-six shooter had pinpointed an enemy bunker position.

Gerun spotted four other bunker positions before a nearby explosion sent his head back down in fear of being disconnected from its neck.

What good was his C-gun, his ziv grenades, or his goff-gas canister in the presence of five or more entrenched bunkers firing really sophisticated weaponry? This was an army Gerun, and his puny arsenal, couldn't possibly stand up against. Nor was he much consoled by at least three mobiles successfully managing eludes (some skillful drivers, those!)

65

in order to fire-back with rounds from Phase-six shooters and—yes—even with a Frendoc Canon. The Frendoc Canon was an illegal weapon as far as public possession. That might explain why it had taken a bit longer for its owner to decide to put it into play. Now, however, there could be little doubt in anyone's mind that this was a life-and-death struggle. Better a Frendoc-Canon owner later fined and jailed for illegal possession, the extenuating circumstances taken into account, than a dead Frendoc-Canon owner without his weapon having been fired in self-defense even once.

One enemy bunker got a canon shot dead-center. The resulting smells added themselves to the over-all stenchy. Gerun literally cheered when another canon shot was lobbed toward yet another enemy position, although this time falling short.

The enemy wasn't slow in realizing there was potential, from the left-over convoy segments, for screwing up the works. Gerun could just imagine the expressions on those unknown faces when they'd first realized it was an honest-to-goodness Frendoc Canon suddenly returning their fire. The poor schmuck in possession of the illegal weapon had invited death from the first moment he'd started firing—possibly another reason he'd been so slow in taking the initiative. A canon was simply something the enemy couldn't afford to let pick them off one at a time.

In one synchronized effort, the remaining bunkers focused Cylic-blazer weave on the threatening mobile spitting canon shot. It was a frighteningly beautiful shroud that first missed its mark, part of its deadly tapestry ripping away, beneath a new spurt of canon fire, then regrouping for another try.

It was obviously soon going to be the end of the valiant Frendoc-Canon, but the concentration of enemy fire on that target allowed Gerun and several other survivors to take full advantage of what little chance was given them for getting back at their attackers. Gerun lined up a bunker in the sights of his C-gun and squeezed off the release trigger. Four other weapons had luckily been lined up on the same target, so Gerun experienced the exhilarating illusion that it was his lone C-gun blast which dissolved a portion of the rock formation and tumbled a Cylic blazer through the breach. The Cylic blazer was on automatic fire as it tumbled, its weave *almost* encompassing Gerun. What a dumbly ironic way that would have been for him to go!

By now, Gerun had a somewhat better grasp of his situation. The convoy wasn't dying without fight-back, two of the enemy bunkers having bitten the dust as a result. However, the odds had always been, and continued to be, in the enemy's favor. Where Gerun had originally counted only five Cylic-blazers, he now realized there'd been a sixth in backup. It had immediately taken up blaze-weaving as soon as its companion piece had toppled through the breach in the bunker wall. The last of the mobiles of the convoy were being picked off like dinols in an f-gun gallery.

Gerun began contemplating a faster retreat. Something he should probably have been contemplating from the start, since it had always been a foregone conclusion that his side wasn't going to win. If the firing of the illegal Frendoc Canon had flooded him with false hope, he should have known better. He would have a far better chance of sneaking away while the battle still raged, than of making any similar attempt during the enemy's leisurely mop-up operations. Still, the idea of running didn't set at all well. No matter that his false sense of the heroic, in not deserting such brave companions on the battlefield, might well be the death of him.

He took a quick account of his mobile, or what was left of it. It wasn't going to take him anywhere, having suffered more damage after he'd jettisoned from it. It was no easy blow to take that his Tilinian cubes were heat-melded to the wreckage and wouldn't be coming with him. He'd been counting on that once-financial-ace-in-the-hole to buy him out of future tough spots. The destruction of his vehicle had, also, deprived him of his reserves of food and drink. If he wasn't yet dead, he wasn't in any too good a shape. On the other hand, the best test of a man was in how he made the best of his circumstances.

He crawled belly-wise along the ground until he'd put a small rise between him and the nearest bunker. He came to a crouch position, and ran like a wasbat out of ledheat. His wasn't a straight run, because of the debris which obstructed any such direct line of retreat. One such pile of scrap, the rear of a mobile whose front had landed elsewhere, offered momentarily concealment while he caught his breath.

There were still spurts of fired weapons above and around him, but not many of them, and none obviously aimed at him. In the interims between firings, there was a disturbing silence. Gerun kept expecting to see wounded or dying, but those people he did see were obviously dead. It was an eerie and unsettling feeling to be the only seeming life in a newly-made graveyard. Everything and everyone about him reeked of mistakes made and not easily corrected.

It was darker now that the weave of deadly laze-weaves no longer competed with the light of Kan-ran-9's three moons. The bluish bathe of Mithric Moon was a gloomy twilight in comparison to the man-made pyrotechnics of mere minutes before.

Gerun heard new sounds and dared peek over the serrated edge of metal-meld. Whoever they were, they were out to gather in the spoils of their night's work, prepared for the job with sal-pods whose extended pinchers and torch-jets unwound metal jigsaws for whatever prizes remained locked within. What would they wonder when Gerun's fused mobile trunk revealed a bonanza of Tilinian? Would they find that any more suspicious than their having been fired upon by a Frendoc Canon hidden illegally within the convoy?

So, where to now? What Gerun still needed was a deep hole, at least one deep enough to keep him out of sight. Hiding within the rubble would only see him soon the victim of pinchers and torch-jets, depending, of course, upon whether the winners considered they had plenty of time in which to conduct their scavenging. Surely, someone in the convoy, with more smarts and better reflexes than Gerun, had been able to transmit a general ZOZ for intercept. Would the receivers have believed Cylic blazers on the offensive, or laughed it off as some kind of bad joke? If the message hadn't specified

Cylic blazers, any investigatory unit was liable to fare no better than the convoy. Cylic blazers simply weren't weapons anyone expected to find outside a military arsenal.

Was the military in revolt? Whoever, there were certainly enough of them. What had initially appeared to be four or five sal-pods had quickly become over ten, the tips of two more appearing over the lip of one bunker.

If there were no convenient holes, Gerun thought he spotted potential for hiding within the ragged rock-face of a stone landscape slab not too far distance. There was evidence of pocket-shadows which he could only hope wouldn't be emptied by the moons shifting above him.

He moved, expecting at any moment to get disintegrated to a crisp. If all that the sal-pods showed visibly were pinchers and torch-jets, Gerun didn't doubt but that they came fully equipped with mechanics that could handle him as easily as any mutilated mobile could be unwound.

He found a pocket-shadow and tried to merge with it. Too small a pool of darkness and, once again, he wished he had less of the muscled physique which was his by right of the Missionary gene bank. Two other pocket-shadows failed to give him sufficient cover, either. Finally, and none too soon, he felt the coolness of complete engulfment and pressed his sweating back flush against rough stone wall.

He needed a mentat-calm. He was breathing too hard and too audibly in the face of sal-pod mechanics which would undoubtedly be monitoring for survivor life-signs. His heartbeat was way off normal.

His legs, which had gotten him this far, were threatening to drop him, for sure. His hands were trembling so badly that he would have slopped sustenance-infused liquid if he'd tried to drink from the jan-lic container secured to his belt.

Needing mentat-calm or not, he couldn't summon it. He was too busy concentrating on the mop-up operations of the enemy, and on his vulnerability. He might have attempted ritual, except shutting his eyes didn't presently appeal to him. He preferred looking death straight in the eye, and dropping to his knees would have emerged a third of his body from pocket-shadow. He couldn't risk that kind of exposure, even for communion with Jon Missionary's God.

He watched and listened, more fearful when the sal-pod occupants became more brazen and began to exit for a bit of informal exploration on their own. It wasn't until a couple such scavengers came really close that Gerun finally recognized their facial features and uniform insignias.

They were Westicks. Westicks with Cylic blazers, no less! Westicks brazen enough to attack a convoy this close to the City. Warluck must have given them a major Tilinian surplus for them to have secured themselves such expensive weaponry and the audacity it took to fire it. It would serve Warluck right if he'd financed his own downfall by fiss-poisoning the clan Missionary.

Gerun's reverie was interrupted by two Westicks grunts of surprised satisfaction that seemed to insinuate detection of him among the shadows. He raised his C-gun, carefully not letting its barrel catch and reflect moons' moonlight, and suddenly realized the two Westicks were concentrating elsewhere. They moved quickly off to his right; he lowered his C-gun and hoped they hadn't spotted his movement.

What they *had* spotted was someone less lucky than Gerun, who—unbeknownst to Gerun—had arrived shortly before him to seek safety among the same pocket-shadows.

"What have we here!" one of the Westicks asked sarcastically, his partner pulling the hider from concealment. The survivor had come through the battle less well than Gerun. The guy's right arm hung limp at his side; his face was bruised, battered, bloody, and bewildered.

"Leftovers," one Westicks said with an accompanying laugh of pure cruelty.

"Please!" the survivor pleaded.

Amid more Westicks's laughter, Gerun raised his C-gun, although there would be little doubt where his shot came from. At the same instant, his pocket-shadow drained its darkness, but not because of shifting moonlight.

Gerun's head jerked in the direction of the find-light suddenly aimed directly at him. He fired.

There was a blinding flash, followed by total darkness.

Gerun's head hurt, his stomach ached, his legs buckled.

CHAPTER SIX

"You seem surprised, my young friend."

"Surely, you didn't expect otherwise."

"Come now, Pylo, consider to whom you're speaking."

"I don't understand."

"No? Then, perhaps, we should end this conversation before it goes any farther. You will, of course, have to deny ever having seen what I've shown you. *I* shall certainly deny its existence."

"I apologize if I've offended."

"Shall we proceed, then?"

"It's just that it's so incredible!"

"Is it, Pylo? Ah, don't frown. It's just that your masquerade is out of place here. Surely, you don't believe any of us got as far as the Religio-College by actually believing Sillona-Xi caused the Bendu Plague, because She'd been short-changed on the drought-reduced harvest at Kistol; or, that Raglistim collapsed a mountain in the Bytamax Province of Rhinic, because workers were too slow in clearing His grotto at Hypernum."

"No?"

"No! Oh, for the congregations, you may give lip service. But no need before your equals. And you may consider me your equal, Pylo, for I have great things in store for you. In time."

"But this evidence insinuates non-existence of Kanran-9 as the universal epi-center."

"It insinuates nothing. It states fact."

"But—"

"We are *not,* nor is Kanran-9, the living center of an otherwise dead universe, it would seem. You know that, I know that, our illustrious brethren of the Religio-College know that. For certain. It is the rest from whom we must worry about keeping this truth a secret. Common man would have trouble adjusting to the idea that he's no more than a drop in a mighty ocean, no more than sludge at the bottom of a barrel of miklona, not the creamer he assumes."

"But Jon Missionary is a half-wit."

"Ah, but before the Xeon brain-blank, what was he? What before he mistook watria for uncontaminated liquid (and that, by the way, is how I heard the story told), allowing the Xeons to gain their advantage?"

"Would an alien being have made that mistake?"

"Kanranians are Kanranian-bound. You answer me: if not from an alien, from where the book?"

—Recording 20-6-R4IX.
Conversation between Panrun-Ru and
Panrun-Ru-II (AKA Pylo Winchest).
Date: 16-2-4-0. Time: 1:1:3.
Security Clearance: FNOEBM.

"WHERE AM I?" It wasn't what Gerun planned to utter. Nor would he have uttered it had he had time to think it over. It was too much the stereotype asked in all the entertainment recordos. It had, however, been a spontaneous slip of his tongue upon opening his eyes to new and strange surroundings. It was not, he knew, the slaughter-house battleground he remembered.

"Castle Thorntown," was the unexpected reply from an unexpected source. As phased-out as Gerun was, he'd wrongly assumed he was totally alone. *She* became more clearly focused only as she bent directly over him.

She put her cool hand on his forehead, saying, "Thank the gods you're conscious."

"Castle Thorntown," he muttered. He was missing a large chunk of his liv-time.

"Can you walk?" she asked, appearing exceedingly nervous. "Are you injured, externally or internally?"

"A phsi-phsis might better tell," Gerun reminded. "There wouldn't be one handy, would there?"

"Ours is executed," the girl replied. "The Westicks's phsi-phsis has proclaimed you fit except for the syrongin inject."

"What syrongin inject?"

"You're lucky it wasn't fiss. It would have been, too, if you'd not shown your true eye."

"My true eye?" He wasn't following the conversation. Hadn't he been hiding in a pocket-shadow made light by the glare of a find? He'd malfunctioned the find, hadn't he? And what of the other survivors?

"Blue," she said. "Seen by the find. For that, and that alone, they substituted the syrongin for fiss. The brown-hue lens of your other eye was recognized after that. You'd apparently lost its companion in the heat of battle."

"Who are you?" Gerun asked, sitting up in pain. His muscles were cramped. He ached. His mouth was dry, his eyes scratchy. What were the aftereffects of syrongin? He tried to remember.

"I'm Tyra-G. And you? Are you really a Missionary?"

"Gerun Missionary," he confirmed. No point in denying. He too well fit the description.

"Of Sira and Kerald issue?" Tyra-G asked.

"You know my tree?" Gerun responded curiously.

"Know it? I'm part of it," Tyra-G surprised. "Although my line, non-Missionary, divert with Rea-Cwan."

"The same Rea-Cwan who was sister of Melina-Lu." It wasn't a question.

"The same," Tyra-G confirmed. "No blue eyes here."

"And what brings the two of us here, descendant of Rea-Cwan?"

"Our bloodlines have saved us both for this moment," Tyra-G said, brushing a stray lock of crilic-colored hair from her forehead. "It's now up to us to save ourselves. Luckily, you've not slept your chance away, although you may desire to stay here to advantage whatever *that* additional delay might give you."

76

"Is my brain completely muddled, or do you speak in riddles?" Gerun asked. Was his splitting headache hampering in-put?

"So little time," she bemoaned, glancing at her wrist-indicator. "You might have been better off to sleep through my departure and not be forced into making the choice for yourself. Madron-Fate often makes the best selections for us."

He would have asked her if it wasn't Madron-Fate who'd caused him to gain consciousness, but clan Missionary had jettisoned that particularly arcane goddess, along with all the rest, when Jon Missionary brought them better.

"I need a briefing," Gerun said. "Decisions are seldom well-made without the facts."

Tyra-G glanced, once again, at her wrist-indicator, her young face screwing up in obvious worry about the time-line.

"I need bye soon," she said with a sigh that expanded and, then, contracted breasts exceedingly well developed for her apparent young age. So many *town noblese* could be traced back to the eight daughters of Maxlima II, it was difficult for Gerun to sort this particular one from the bunch. Hardly *Prime Noblese,* since Thorntown was hardly Prime-town Category. Minor-noblese, then, but still very pretty.

"Any detail is better than none," Gerun assured her.

"You were in convoy," Tyra-G said. "There was a Westicks raid. You were spotted as a Missionary—"

"One blue eye spotted by the find?"

"Exactly," Tyra-G confirmed. "Lucky for you, because the Westicks took no other prisoners."

"None?"

"None. And here, in Thorntown—" She visibly shivered. "—I can't begin to count the numbers terminated."

"Yet, *you* live. Alone?"

"Low-grade are terminated. Minor-grade are saved for ransom. Think the Westicks, anyway. My father thinks otherwise; he anticipated the Westicks's move and planned for it, no matter—yes, or no—the Religio-College decision to ransom."

"Planned how?"

"Escape," Tyra-G whispered. "Ruler of a border town, my father heard rumors of Westicks's munitions purchases and suspected they would move against us first. He made arrangements. Had you delayed consciousness longer, I would have been gone when you awoke. As it is, you must make the decision as to come or stay."

"You actually think I'd entertain staying?" Gerun asked. That *was* what she'd been insinuating.

"There's no question but that the Religio-College *will* ransom *you*. They'd sent out unofficial queries prior to this Westicks's raid. The Westicks have seen the transcripts and, as brewers of fiss poisoning, are aware of the Religio-College's desire for you. Thus, your survival from the doomed convoy. I wouldn't be as anxious to get where *I'm* finally going if I were in your shoes."

"You know of the Religio-College's purge of my clan, then?" For some reason, that surprised him. Whenever clan members *had* made suggestions that they were being prejudiced against by the Religio-College, there'd been accusations of acute paranoia.

"Many know," Tyra-G surprised further. "Many care less. Your clan's loss of power and greatness leaves power and greatness to be absorbed by others. Even my father, who is more generous than most, has labeled you and yours as an arrogant branch, and he has done so on more than one occasion."

"We have been systematically eliminated from twenty-four to two!" Gerun reminded, aghast. "While there were those who knew but stood idly by?"

"*Better them than us* was always the winning argument whenever I heard mention of any possible assist to you and yours brought up by those locked in chamber. And if the Religio–College has so much clout they can take on the clan Missionary and succeed, what chances have we, in far-from-the-hub places like Thorntown, of swimming against the flow?"

"Those who sat and watched will soon enough see themselves the victims while others stand idly by."

Tyra-G shrugged. "The argument is best made with those who count. I'm but one daughter of no say. I hold no sway in chamber. I couldn't have saved one Missionary his fate, even had I put up the effort. I can save *you* for only a brief moment by offering you a means to escape, here and now. But for you that escape is nothing more than a faster route to the City than might be achieved by you waiting here for the ransom amount to be decided upon to the satisfaction of the Westicks. Of course, by escaping with me now, you could later escape me."

"To go where?" It was a question he had meant to ask only himself. He wasn't pleased it had slipped out.

"Go where you were headed when you were forced upon this detour," Tyra-G suggested.

She couldn't know he'd had no particular destination in mind at the time. He'd been running blind, as he was still running blind. Shagtown had been a place picked off the top of his head to fill the curiosity of the Thorntown man in the convoy ahead of him. The man had never made it to Thorntown; Gerun had. There was bitter irony in there somewhere.

"Yes, I'm safer with you than with the Westicks," Gerun decided.

"It would be unfair, however, for me to suggest you'll be traveling in friendly company," Tyra-G warned. "Tree-related or not."

"Oh?" What was she getting at? She'd seemed friendly enough, more clearly defining his prospects than his own muddled brain had been able to do.

"My father is a good man," Tyra-G argued, "but he leaves much behind in Thorntown that he was unable to get out before us. He likely doesn't welcome his prospects for a new start in the City to where he now flees in exile. Bringing with him Gerun Missionary in offering could be the key to open many doors for him, especially in a time when so many minor-noblese flee to the City to escape warring Westicks. Ransom need not always be paid in Tilinian as the Westicks would have it, you know? It could come in the form of elevating minor above minor."

80

"Your father would barter me for position? But we're tree," Gerun protested.

"You seen as an arrogant tree part that has grown fat and wealthy while my father needed to be content with the likes of Thorntown. He owes you and yours nothing. You, on the other hand, perhaps, owe him a chance to succeed where you failed. It's but a word to the wise. How can I know for sure how he will react when he sees you along for the ride?"

"He doesn't expect me, then?"

"I've not talked or seen him since our separate confinements. The plan we follow was laid down ages ago when he first feared Westicks's movement across our border. It's not something we've worked out by tapping out messages through castle plumbing. However, news sometimes travels mysteriously via invisible communications lines. It could well be that he *does* expect you. It could well be that Warluck and the Religio-College expect you, too, whether delivered by Westicks or by Banic of Thorntown."

"It seems that I have much to thank you for," Gerun said, mentat-commanding his aching head be still. There were bells ringing all too loudly between his ears. "Tell me more of your escape plan."

Tyra-G glanced nervously round the room. Expecting bugging? Why not? Except she had already committed herself enough so that the Westicks should have been barging entrance before now. Unless they were holding fast for specifics, the likes of which Gerun had so carelessly asked.

"Maybe it would be safer to refrain from giving me specifics until we're on the way?" Gerun suggested diplomatically.

He heard the massive bolts on the door being thrown. In unison, Tyra-G and he turned to see ten Westicks soldiers, fully uniformed and armed, burst into the room.

CHAPTER SEVEN

"Then, it was merely a holding action."

"Precisely. The book incinerate, I felt, I could risk, and I did. But the man was another aspect, all together. The hot-blooded little princess took a shine to him. What with Geulin named co-conspirator in the assassination attempt on the life of Maxlima II, the Religio-College wasn't standing on the power base it once did. I rightly suspected Maxlima II would flex his muscle by going against us, just because he could. Luckily, I maneuvered him, with the unknowing assistance of Melina-Lu, into surrendering the book, if not the man. The book seemed the more dangerous threat to us at the time. After all, Jon Missionary was mentally unstable and seemingly less dangerous. Were he to have regained his senses, his destruction would have taken precedence, of course, as it would even to this day. We're best able to act successfully, however, once we've regained the more solid power base which, I suspect, won't be ours until long after Jon Missionary has passed into his grave."

"Which is why you've show me this?"

"Exactly. I needed to assure your cooperation, as you may need to assure the cooperation of those chosen to follow you. Because Jon Missionary's gene bank *does* remain a threat to us. Already the woman is attributing aspects of religion to his garble. Who knows what mystical interpretations will evolve via her children and her children's children? He's a foreign element that taints everything that comes near him, as his mumbo-jumbo taints. We must bide our time until the right time—whether in your lifetime or in the lifetime of the one or ones who follow you—when the Religio-College is once again a power with which to be reckoned. At that time, there *must* be one of us to take action."

"As you would have acted—had you been able?"

"We are not of his gene bank. Is it wise to let that power go to the Noblese? Already the woman is turned mystic, making something of nothing. Whether genuine or synthesized merely to rationalize her desire for the half-wit, it's a threat that *must* be dealt with."

"If the power comes within my lifetime, I'll take appropriate action."

"I knew I could trust you. But if the power base isn't yet strong enough by the time you step down...."

"My successor will be prepared, having seen the evidence, as you have prepared me, and will be prepared to take the necessary actions."

"And that is how it must be, from successor to successor, until...."

"Until the corruption is with us no longer."

"Amen!"

GERUN, THE HERETIC, BY WILLIAM MALTESE

—Recording 20-6R4IV.
Conversation between Panrun-Ru and
Panrun-Ru II (AKA Pylo Wincrest).
Date 16-2-4-0. Time: 1:2:4.
Security Clearance: FNOEBM.

THE WESTICKS SOLDIERS parenthesized the room, the last two positioned by the door through which the Westicks officer entered.

"Mishin Morg," Tyra-G whispered, and Gerun wondered if she'd spoken for his benefit or involuntarily in response to the danger. Mishin Morg's timing was well enough so that it insinuated he'd overheard the preceding conversation. If that were the case, Gerun's chance of escape was aborted almost as quickly as it had been presented.

"Tyra-G, this *is* a surprise," said Mishin Morg and actually seemed genuinely surprised. While Westicks cheekbones were higher, noses larger, chins less predominant than those of the Rylons, their faces' musculature relayed emotions nearly as well.

"A surprise?" asked Tyra-G. To Gerun, she seemed to be handling the catastrophic situation quite well. The nervousness she'd shown with him was well masked for the occasion.

"You'll admit that the last time I saw you, you weren't occupying this particular space. I'd arrived here, thinking only to see the Missionary."

"Well, you weren't the only one who was curious to see him," Tyra-G said. "He is, after all, tree through the sister of my ancestor, Rea-Cwan.

"A kinship I would think you reluctant to admit in the face of the recent purge on the clan Missionary."

"Purge?" Tyra-G asked, all innocence. "Perhaps, you would be so kind as to tell me *what* purge, instigated by whom?"

"I think, rather, you should tell me how you came to be here when there are guards who still line the hallway in the belief that you're in confinement within the room adjoining."

Gerun knew there was no way Mishin would slip further into revealing just how official the Religio-College's unofficial purge of the clan Missionary really had become. If Mishin and the Westicks were moving against the Religio-College and the Rylon Rulers, he wasn't yet firmly enough entrenched to risk revealing information given him in the strictest confidence. A man who couldn't keep secrets was little respected by those who could.

"My passage from there to here was easy," Tyra-G replied airily. She'd not pressed for more details on the purge. It had been enough that Mishin had slipped, and Tyra-G had called him to task for it. To have pressed for more advantage would have been a dangerous step in the face of her predicament. After all, it was highly unlikely that, despite Mishin's efforts, there would be any funds found for her ransom. Warluck had already poured overly much revenue into the Westicks's coffers in his efforts to destroy the clan Missionary. It wouldn't take an overextension of Warluck's wiles to persuade Ruellin VI that the minor-noblese of this and other border towns were pawns to be sacrificed in the war. After all, rewards would be needed to disburse to those loyal fighters in the clash, and what better rewards to offer them than rank vacated in terminations of the oh-so-cruel enemy which had been defeated?

"You came via door?" Mishin asked, his hairy eyebrow lifting to a v above his pin-pointy drancolored eyes. He walked to the only other door in the room and tried the locked catch. "You wear a key around your neck that wasn't there when last I searched you?"

Gerun read Tyra-G's blush as indication of the indignation she'd already suffered beneath the paw-like hands of the brute, but her voice was calm enough as she answered.

"There are locked doors, and then there are doors locked," she said, walking to the wall a few steps to Mishin's right and hand-pressing a hidden catch. A slab of seemingly sold pestic slid upward, with nary a sigh, revealing the room on the other side.

Mishin's surprise was laughable. It took all of Gerun's willpower, in the face of his own amazement, to keep from bursting into hearty guffaws.

"This room was checked for concelos!" Mishin insisted, apparently still disbelieving the opening she showed him.

"Obviously, by men little adept at their work," Tyra-G chided. "I hope them the exceptions rather than the rule if you hope to be final victor in any war."

"How many other concelos lie overlooked within the castle walls?" Mishin asked. Whether it was a question he'd asked himself or asked Tyra-G was hard to tell. Tyra G answered him, nonetheless.

"Hardly enough of them," she said, "or, by now, I would be outside the walls and not merely next door."

Gerun could read the visible relief Mishin experienced. The Westicks's emotions were all too readily visible. It was something to remember when dealing with him in the future.

"Nevertheless, I think a reprimand is invited on those whom overlooked even this harmless opening," he said.

"By all means," Tyra-G agreed. "The firmer the reprimand, the better." Her sarcasm continued: "Perhaps, too, another run-through of the castle for loopholes?"

Gerun wondered if the escape route she'd mentioned to him had required their exit through some other secret door, soon to be secret no longer.

She'd been constantly checking her wrist indicator before Mishin's arrival. Had she missed whatever the connection she'd been waiting for?

"In the meantime, I would like a little discussion with the Missionary alone," Mishin said. "So, since you've reopened this door of yours, why not oblige me further by walking on through it?"

"Your company has never been so wondrous that I would argue a request to leave it," Tyra-G said, glided through the opening, and closed it from the other side, behind her, all before Mishin could come up with a retort.

"Leave us!" Mishin commanded his guards, his temper little improved by Tyra-G's parting remarks. "Sit!" he commanded Gerun when the room was empty except for the two of them, all doors shut.

Gerun sat, and Mishin remained standing. Apparently, the Westicks was fully aware of the psychological advantage to the dominance of his standing position in regard to Gerun's sitting one.

"Shall you thank me for my clan's part in inadvertently financing your rebellion?" Gerun asked, luxuriating in the confusing expressions *that* brought to Mishin's face. "Come now," Gerun encouraged, "why can't we be frank since there are only the two of us and no one else to carry the tale?"

"Castle walls with secret doors can conceal secret ears," Mishin predicted, reminding Gerun that the fears he'd had of *Mishin's* hidden ears had apparently been wrong. In that, surely, had Mishin overheard Tyra-G's whispers of escape, he wouldn't have passed them over, as he had up until now. So, more likely as not, it had been coincidence which had materialized the Westicks on the immediate tail of Tyra-G's revelations. Mishin's obvious surprise to see her with Gerun only proved the same.

"I have nothing to fear from secret ears," Gerun said bravely. And, in fact, what *did* he have to fear from them? "So, let me tell you what I know of the Westicks's stockpile of munitions bought with the death of my fellow clan members."

"Don't forget your *own* death's soon-contribution to the kitty," Mishin added, apparently deciding to be more candid that he'd originally intended. "I figure what I'm paid ransom for you will add at least two more Cylic blazers to my arsenal."

"And you think me dead at the hands of the Religio-College, you with two additional Cylic blazers, outweighs the advantages of you keeping me alive, here?" Gerun asked.

"Alive you are but one more mouth for me to feed, an opportunity lost if you were ever to escape me."

"The same incompetence that overlooked hidden doorways will one day overlook me, you mean?" Gerun mocked.

90

"Yes, maybe," Mishin admitted angrily, pacing this way and that.

"But if the Religio-College tries so hard to kill me, what an ace-in-your-sleeve to keep them from it," Gerun argued.

"Only until they wake up to the fact that you're no more of a threat to them than the rest of your clan has ever been," Mishin argued in return. "Then, I'm out two Cylic blazers, aren't I?"

"Having killed so many Missionaries to prove their point, do you actually foresee them ever seeing me as a lessened threat?" Gerun asked. In the hands of Warluck, his death was a certainty. On the other hand, if he could convince Mishin to hold on to him...

"I've shown them a taste of what their paranoia has bought them," Mishin bragged. "I've amassed an army to threaten them, purchased by their own funds. I've captured not just Thorntown, but Shag-town, Psyetown, Grintown, and Moultown, as well as smaller outlying settlements. All because some-one out there fears that Jon Missionary taught of some kind of new god to challenge the very exis-tence of all the gods within the Religio-College pan-theon. Poppycock! Your ancestor was a raving luna-tic. You know that, I know that, the Religio-College will wake up to that fact once they've seen what mischief they've allowed by believing otherwise."

"They fear Jon Missionary's god?" Gerun tried to make it a statement but didn't succeed.

"Does not the Religio-College, by definition, deal with the gods?" Mishin reminded. "Oh, granted, they deal in power and politics, too, espe-cially with an incompetent like Ruellin VI as Ruler, but they really weren't expecting clan Missionary to rise up in arms—ever. So why do *you* think they instigated their purge?"

"There *was* a purge, then?" Gerun asked and missed the perfect opportunity to ask *why?* of someone who might know the answer for certain.

Mishin smiled slyly. His beady eyes became more so.

"Who told you Religio-College Tilinian was passing into Westicks's hands?" he asked.

"Missionaries were dying of fiss poisoning," Gerun said. "Who brews the poison in such quantities as Westicks? Who could afford the massive doses necessary but Warluck?"

"Who told you it was fiss poisoning?" Mishin asked. "The deaths of your clan members were well orchestrated as natural-seeming, under most circumstances. The masquerades were complete enough to belie suspicion. Yet, *you* seem to have easily enough put two and two together. Why do I find that mental dexterity far too superior for a snot-nosed boy?"

"Yes, but this snot-nosed boy has the god of Jon Missionary behind him, doesn't he?"

Mishin surprised with a mighty laugh, rumbling with genuine humor. He wiped tears of mirth from his beady eyes.

"Only an ignorant kid, indeed, would assume to threaten me with the god-card dealt via the babblings of a half-wit," Mishin managed between additional chuckles. "I have no belief in your god, boy! I have no believe in *any* god. If I did, do you think I would be taking on the religious heads within the Religio-College's pantheon, in the face of the excommunications already being tossed in my direction? If I mouth the notion that my war is meant to throw off the yoke of religious men grown more intent upon fattening their purses than serving their gods, that's only pap for my followers who need to believe in more than Mishin Morg. I will tell you one thing, however. If I *did* believe, it would never be in the god of Jon Missionary, half-wit. And unless the Religio-College holds some bit of evidence they're not sharing with me, or with anyone else, they've been fools to finance me and mine to the end of ending clan Missionary. I've the ability to fight such fools and win. Watch me. In fact, I'm tempted to keep you around, alive, here, just to see how easily I dispose of the same group that has brought you and yours to the brink of extinction. *Except* only a fool would choose you in the pick between you and Cylic blazers. And the only fools in this war are on my other side."

"You're a fool if you think so," Gerun warned, and Mishin slapped him. The force of the blow knocked Gerun from his seat.

"You're the only fool in this room," Mishin accused, standing triumphantly over him. "One of the last in a whole clan of fools who were so busy fabricating a god to their own glory that they left themselves vulnerable to attack from the very gods they meant theirs to supplant."

"I think the clan Missionary and the Religio-College know something that will be your downfall for not knowing," Gerun warned with a good deal more bravura than he felt. His head still reeled from the blow Mishin's ham-like paw had delivered, not to mention the still-continued ringing as aftermath of his debilitating syrongin inject.

"Of course, *you* think it," Mishin mocked. "You *must* think it or face the less than attractive alternative that you're the product not of some celestial union between prophet and princess but of a rut between a half-wit and the demented woman who lusted after him.

"We'll see," Gerun said, trying to sound confident. This was difficult to do from his subservient sprawl on the floor.

"Get up!" Mishin commanded. "You bore me. I bore easily in the company of a fool."

Mishin walked to the point on the wall where Tyra-G had so recently exited. He fumbled for the release catch so cleverly hidden that he had difficulty finding it, even though he knew full well that it was there. His face was red with frustration by the time the door finally slid open for him.

"Shall we have the little lady help you to your feet?" Mishin asked, obviously amused by Gerun's less-than-successful efforts to resume a standing position. "Tyra-G!" he shouted. "Come in here and give your precious kin, Chosen of God, a helping hand. He seems to have trouble managing on his own."

Mishin Mog laughed, his laugh converting to a scowl when it continued to be only him watching Gerun's struggles.

"Tyra-G!" he shouted louder and plunged through the opening to fetch her.

Using the back of a chair, Gerun managed to get to his feet. His head still rang with the blow and lingering syrongin. His vision was swimming, but not enough so that he didn't know, without being told, upon Mishin's return to the room, that Tyra-G had made good her escape and was gone.

Mishin didn't miss the satisfied expression on Gerun's face, either.

"A pity your girl friend didn't take you with her," Mishin said, his beady eyes bright with anger, "because I plan to make you pay for her cleverness in *trying* to escape me. And, yes, I *do* emphasize *trying*. She'll be mine again before she's out of the castle."

Gerun shuddered, and Mishin called for his guards.

CHAPTER EIGHT

"He is risen!"
"More likely, the grave is robbed!"

—Syurilla and Paul Missionary,
upon discovering the open
grave of Jon Missionary.

"PLEASE, NO!" GERUN BEGGED, barely having the strength to manage even that.

"Up, boy, up!" someone commanded. "We have very little time for this."

The longer the delay of Gerun's return to the tortu-chamber, the better for him, was how Gerun saw things. He'd been drained by the sessions Mishin and that man's goons had already put him through. Did they think he had something more to tell them that he hadn't already told? Well, they were mistaken. He'd spilled his guts. Telling them about Kalvin (thank God, he hadn't known where his grandfather was holed up!). Telling them about Tyra-G's offer of escape (thank God, he hadn't allowed her to go into specifics!). He had nothing else to tell. Although he doubted Mishin would take that as an argument to postpone another session. Nor listen to the argument that more torture would see Warluck receiving damaged goods. *"Warluck will care little for the condition of someone he merely means to kill himself,"* Mishin would merely, and rightly, remind. There were men who thoroughly enjoyed witnessing the suffering of others, and Mishin was obviously of the breed.

"I can't and won't move!" Gerun insisted. How long had Mishin sparkled pain along Gerun's nerve ends before Gerun had blacked out, this last time? Too long. *Way* too long. The prospect of repeating the endurance test left Gerun fearful and sweating.

"You must try, Gerun Missionary!" someone insisted. A woman? There had been no women in the tortu-chamber, although Gerun bet there *were* Westicks women who'd relish the spectacle.

97

"I can give him some support, but he'll have to help himself, too," a third voice said.

There was little point in Gerun resisting. They seemed intent upon moving him.

"Maybe, we'd better leave without him." Who suggested that? The woman? Why did the woman's voice sound familiar?

"If only we could get him through," someone said. Through what? He had already been *through* more than he'd ever thought possible to go *through*.

"*Through* isn't enough," the woman reminded. Tyra-G? No, it wasn't possible. She was gone. She'd escaped. Mishin's timing had prevented Gerun from taking similar advantage.

"She's right," someone confirmed. "Once he's found missing, they'll not stop until the concelo is found. We must be well into the maze by then."

"If only he'd give us some help. By the gods, his muscle is more dead-weight than if he were actually dead."

"Let's *do* leave him, then," the woman argued.

"If only he'd realize we're here to help," the one man said.

Two men and a woman, or was it a girl? Why were they having such a hard time with him? Mishin would only have had to clap his hands, and a whole company of Westicks guards could hoist Gerun and carry him off. Gerun had been little enough trouble for them before now. So, why the big fuss, now?

"We have so little time," someone said. It was hard for Gerun to tell whose voice was whose. Except, of course, there was the female. Girl, if it were Tyra-G. Was it Tyra-G? Knowing nothing of her escape plans, had he spilled some secret anyway, so

Mishin had found her and brought her back? Mishin had warned she'd never get beyond the castle walls. Had he made good on his threat, just as he'd made good on his threat to make Gerun pay for the girl's disappearance.

"Tyra-G?" he asked. If they had her, he wasn't sure he wanted to regain consciousness to see what they planned to do to her—or to him. Is that what they wanted him revived to see?

"Yes, it's Tyra-G," one man confirmed. "She's brought us back to help you, boy. But we can't help you unless you help us help you. You've got to walk. Not far but far enough to lose the Westicks in the maze once they've located the concelo into it."

Mishin already knew about the concelo separating Gerun's room from the room of Tyra-G. Except Gerun wasn't in that room any longer, was he? He was in the castle's lower honeycomb. In a cell. Dumped there when Mishin had last finished with him—for the moment. *There'll be plenty more fun-times before I turn you over to Warluck,* Mishin had promised. *I'll have you as half-wit as your august relative, Jon Missionary, by the time I'm through with you.*

"You must concentrate to coordinate, boy," someone told him. A man. Whose voice Gerun confused uncertainly with Mishin's. Except it wasn't Mishin's voice. Gerun would never forget Mishin's voice. "He hasn't been damaged irrevocably, as far as I can tell," the same man said. Or, was it another one? It was so hard to concentrate.

"You've the track marks of drugs, Gerun Missionary," the woman said. Yes, it was Tyra-G's voice. Poor Tyra-G. Where in the maze had Mishin caught her? "You must merely concentrate on over-riding the residue of them still left in your system," she told him.

"Should we risk an inject of ziphonine?" Who suggested that?

"With everything Mishin injected, it might kill him," the woman warned.

"Would he be any worse off dead?"

Gerun tried to clear his head. He really did try. He was just having an extremely hard time getting his mind around anything.

"I say we try it," someone said.

Try what? Another inject? Another descent into painful horror?

"No!" he protested and jerked his arm away—this time.

"It'll help you function," a man promised.

"It may very well kill him," the woman argued.

"We're running out of time," a man warned.

"Who are you?" Gerun asked. There were three of them, spotted through a fading mist. The woman, the girl, *was* Tyra-G.

"He's caught you," Gerun bemoaned. "Because of something I told him?" He didn't want that burden laid on him. He'd been so determined to keep silent, no matter what. All that fine commitment had gone down the toilet with the first inject Mishin had given him. Before it was over, Gerun would have sold out Jon Missionary, himself, to get release from the pain.

"He's not caught me," Tyra-G said. "I've come back for you. I've brought my father and Minotan. Minotan knows the way out, through the maze."

"But we must hurry," a man insisted. An old man. White beard. White eyes. White skin. "We don't have much time remaining."

"Can you walk?" asked the other man. Middle-aged. Fine head of hair. Tyra-G's coloring. Her father, then? Ruler of Thorntown? No, Mishin was now Ruler of Thorntown.

"I can walk," Gerun insisted. More boasting than truth. His wobbly legs seemed quite rebellious to his efforts to put his weight upon them. He concentrated to put one foot in front of the other. He was making very little progress, even with the help of three people. Where were they so intent upon taking him, anyway?

The gate was open. Not the gate, the wall. The wall was open, showing a black hole where there'd been the illusion of solid stone before. A concelo revealed within his cell?

"A concelo?" he asked.

"Yes," two men and the girl said in unison.

They were offering him escape. All he had to do was muster the steam to walk out of the exit they'd provided. He couldn't muff this. He just couldn't. Thinking of what awaited him in alternative gave him added incentive.

"Yes, yes," Minotan encouraged. "Only a little farther."

Gerun tried a mentat-run-through, having more success than when he'd tried one in the tortu-chamber to counteract the pain. In the tortu-chamber, his mentat-exercise abilities seemingly deserted him. Now, they were back, for the moment. He concentrated on the here and now. He mentated on putting reason to the in-feed given. Tyra-G, her

father, an old, blind man, named Minotan. A concelo, leading where? To a maze? Was there safety in
the maze? When they lost Mishin, would they lose
themselves as well?

"Someone is coming," the old man warned. Gerun struggled to hear the same sounds of someone's
approach, but he heard nothing.

"It's now or never, Gerun Missionary," Tyra-G
pronounced. "You must help us save you, or you
must not be saved."

He summoned mentat-reserve, stepping up into
the darkness revealed by the gaping concelo. He
heard the sounds of distant grating of metal against
metal—heard by Minotan long before Gerun's ears
had caught them—just before the concelo dropped
its face and plunged them all into darkness.

"A human chain is required!" Minotan instructed. His voice was the only sound in a darkness
so complete that Gerun couldn't see his own hand
before his own face.

"Banic, touch me, the boy touch Banic, Tyra-G
behind. Ready?"

Someone guided Gerun's hands to the shoulders
in line ahead of him.

"Lock on," Minotan instructed, and Gerun's
fingers curled into a firmer grip.

"I'm locked on," Tyra-G informed, immediately
after Gerun felt her fingers at his waist.

"We move as one, then," the old man said.
"Slowly, at first, until we get the necessary rhythm,
then as fast as conditions allow. There is a straight
stretch, and we'll not be safe until we've rounded
several bends."

It wasn't easy for Gerun to achieve the desired rhythm. His coordination remained off-sync. He stepped on Banic's heels, making Tyra-G step on Gerun's ankle. He stumbled. Twice he fell, and they had to form up again in the darkness.

"Leave me," Gerun said, frustrated upon his third fall. At the same time, he was afraid they *would* leave him. Sounds behind them evidenced the discovery, if not the breaching, of the concelo. If Mishin caught him now....

"We'll leave you when it is a case of our needing to do so to save ourselves," Minotan said. "For the moment, there is still time to save you and us. We have only a few steps more to safety, although many more steps to escape. You must merely try harder to concentrate."

There was a monstrous clanging sound and, behind them, a pinpoint of light in the gloom.

"They're in," Minotan announced calmly. "We must keep moving."

And they did keep moving. And Gerun kept concentrating all of his mentat-reserve to help him move smoothly. With each step, the sounds of their pursuers became louder, until Gerun feared to look back for fear of discovering the enemy right atop him.

"Concentrate as I veer," Minotan warned, his whisper low so that it carried no clue to the noisy pursuers behind them.

Their human serpentine turned, and then turned again. It seemed to Gerun as if they'd merely faced their rear, except there was no sign of light or men. Momentarily, he lost concentration, stubbed his toe and almost went down. Their again interrupted linking paused for another regrouping.

"Just a bit farther," Minotan encouraged. "Although we could stop here, I would feel safer with more bends between us."

"Are you all right, Gerun?" Tyra-G asked from behind him.

"Yes," Gerun said, thinking for the first time that he might very well be.

"Let's move, then," Minotan ordered, and they were off again, more slowly this time.

"Veerings here," came a distant shout from behind.

"How many?" came a distant query.

"Two."

"Halve the company."

"Yes, sir."

Gerun finally felt himself an integral part of this four-headed, eight-legged molein, progressing through black corridors. He began to sense, by their sway, as to which way they would veer next. He no longer stumbled, no longer felt even the urge to stumble. He experienced a revival of the strength the negative drug injects and resulting pain had sapped from him in the tortu-chamber. The heavy gasps of breath, when they came, weren't his but those of Banic, Tyra-G's father, ahead of him.

"We may rest, here," Minotan said. *His* breathing was calm and even.

"Thank the gods," Tyra-G sighed in gratitude. There was a definite breathlessness within her words.

"Disengage and sit, then," Minotan instructed.

Gerun released and was released. He backed against cold stone and slid the wall.

"What is this place?" he asked; the darkness made him seem totally alone.

"The maze," Tyra-G said. "Here long before the castle atop it."

"No light?" Gerun asked. It was, also, a request to have some.

"Our guide doesn't need light," Tyra-G reminded. "His conditions for rescue included we bring none."

"How does he know this place's secrets?" Gerun asked, curious. At the same time, he was prepared to curb his curiosity if objections were raised to his inquiry. He wasn't one to look a gift hornit in the mouthix.

"We were released here in the time of Kis-koff," Minotan said, "as punishment for grave misdeeds. We were scheduled to become lost and die. But lost, we survived. Lost, we bred. Lost, we mapped to locate an exit. But exits, once found, provided access to a world gone mad in our absence. So, we preferred a return to these surroundings to which we'd so completely adapted."

"You live here, then?" Gerun asked, frankly aghast. So dark. But, then, he'd noted the blindness of the man. What was more darkness to one who'd known nothing else?

"Lived her far longer than you've lived, Gerun Missionary," Minotan said. "Far longer than most have lived on the outside."

"There was a cave-in of the maze in a section beneath the castle," Tyra-G said. "Heavy rocks that rested upon less-than-adequate supports gave way and caught. Minotan in the rubble; we rescued him."

"Their rescue is a debt owed," Minotan said. "Now being repaid."

"And *my* rescue?" Gerun asked. What did he have left to offer in payment? His reserve of Tilinian had gone with his mobile.

"We need make the trip through, anyway, so what's one more our number?" Minotan replied graciously. "Best always to overpay a repay, rather than be niggardly is well-said."

"I thank you, then."

"Thank Tyra-G," the old man said. "For it is only through her that we knew of you.

"My thanks, of course, to Tyra-G—and to Banic, her father."

"It is our pleasure, my boy," Banic said. "We're tree, after all, are we not?"

"Aye," Gerun confirmed. "Through Rea-Cwan, sister of Melina-Lu, daughter of Maxlima II."

"Westicks would have little dared their impudence in Maxlima II's time," Banic said.

"I envy you not for your existence beyond the maze," Minotan said.

"We envy you your peacefulness within it," Tyra-G said.

Was peace worth a life forever existed within total darkness?

There was a sudden scream that echoed through the passage, muted by the distance it had to travel. The sound caused a rising of hair along the back of Gerun's neck.

"That one has lost our way and his," Minotan said with satisfaction. "Losing ways is the way of

106

the maze. Me and mine shall have many feasts from this. See, already I'm rewarded for helping you, Gerun Missionary."

Gerun would have questioned the meaning of what Minotan had just said, but Tyra-G's hand was suddenly on his arm and warning him with a squeeze.

There were more sounds of men lost and becoming lost.

"Hear how meals call out to their diners?" Minotan said, smacking his lips.

The chill at Gerun's hairline shivered all of the way to his toes.

CHAPTER NINE

"We were interrupted. Unfortunately."

"But you *were* able to secure his body."

"Yes. But there's no denying it would have been preferable had its removal gone unnoticed by all."

"We've at least met our chief objective."

"And the autopsical analysis?"

"Lab-tech Kapo is going to do it for us in a labo-sec we've specially set up for him in the seclusion of Maxo-built Three. He's waiting there now."

"No need to unload the body, then. We can transport it from storage as is."

"Except for the head."

"The head?"

"Badly decomposed as it is, I recognize its owner, don't you? No need to get Kapo any more concerned than he is already soon to be. There are rumors enough about the clan Missionary without connecting them in anyway to this, especially after the results come in."

"You anticipate the results, then?"

"Can we expect any less shock from the man than from his book?"

GERUN, THE HERETIC, BY WILLIAM MALTESE

—Recording 400-4-Z2II.
Conversation between Panrun-Ru II and
Samtol-Mu VI (AKA Harold Mix).
Date: 44-9-4.
Security Clearance: FNOEBM.

SO LONG A STRETCH OF DARKNESS! A darkness that didn't wane with exposure to it, either. All of this time later, the blackout was as complete as it had been when Gerun had first entered the maze, the concelo face dropping to separate him from his cell.

So many twists and turns. To the left, to the right, this way and that, vortexes leading them down, helixes leading them up. To where? To what? To safety? Gerun certainly hoped it was to safety, because there was little safety in the maze by the wails of the men now lost in it. That those men had been intent upon finding Gerun for his return to the tortu-chamber didn't alleviate the sympathy Gerun now felt for those screams of ways-lost that echoed the blackened passageways. Although the fate of Gerun's pursuers, as hinted to him by Minotan, was not one upon which Gerun wished to linger, considering his own along-for-the-ride status.

"Rest here," Minotan instructed, interrupting a silence previously punctuated only by heavy breathing and footsteps against rock.

"Yes, I could use the break," Banic mumbled, first to break the linkage and first to slide the wall to a sitting position.

"I'll check ahead," Minotan said. "I won't be long."

Beside him, Gerun felt Tyra-G shiver. It was a twin of the shiver inside him. Neither shivered from the cold. The in-maze temperature, in fact, was quite balmy.

Gerun listened for sounds of Minotan's departure but didn't hear any. Some inner feeling, some

110

sense of relief—despite his precarious position without Minotan—informed him that their guide was temporarily gone.

"You say there are more like him who call this place home?" Gerun asked, checking his wrist-indicator for the umpteenth time and wondering what there was about the darkness of this place that shrouded even readout illumination. He hadn't a notion as to the correct time.

"We've never seen others," Tyra-G admitted.

"Certainly, we've seen no physical sign of them," Banic commented, back to regular breathing. "But, then, we could just have walked by all kinds of such evidence and missed it in this gloom."

"Yes," Gerun agreed.

"Do you think Minotan will come back?" Tyra-G asked after a pregnant moment. Gerun sensed a recurrence of chilling throughout him, empathetically emanating from her.

"He could have deserted us long before now, had he a mind to," Banic reminded. "Is there a one of us who has kept his orientation through the twists and turns behind us?"

"Certainly, not I," Tyra-G admitted.

"My concentration was initially upon managing one foot before the other," Gerun confessed.

"Minotan seems an honorable man," Banic consoled. "An honorable man pays his debuts without shirking."

"Besides, our fate here could be no worse than the fate awaiting us at the castle," Tyra-G rationalized.

"Amen," her father concurred.

Minotan interrupted any further conjecture about his return by clearing his throat in warning of his approach.

"How goes our path ahead?" Banic asked.

"Favorable," Minotan assured. "But I must warn you that these next steps require a certain fleetness of foot and a need for exceptional quiet."

"What's the additional danger?" Gerun asked, knowing what had been insinuated.

"The maze has a collapse through here, much as occurred under the castle," Minotan explained. "Only the nature of this collapse has made its repair exceedingly dangerous. Four of mine have already lost their lives in the attempt. Burrowing a new pathway is not within our capabilities. After all, we didn't build the maze but merely make it our home, much as the vulnerable seacreat of my ancestors-before-our-maze-time was myth-sang to have carried no shell of its own but borrowed from those discarded upon the bed of the sea. Only a detour is within our means, here. Dangerous in that it necessitates a momentary return to the outside."

"Where Mishin's men are on the prowl?" Tyra-G injected.

"We are presently far from Mishin's realm of influence," Minotan assured. "However, Mysons, on occasion, can be as dangerous."

"Mysons?" Gerun queried.

"Aye," Minotan confirmed. "It is their world out there. And while they have come to look upon our detour through their space as sacred to their gods, it would be unwise for them to sense our trespass through their mistakenly assumed holy ground. I've sniffed the air, and I've found it clear of Mysons worshipers. I shall sniff again before risking our exposure. A reentry to the maze, I assure you, is not too distant beyond the detour."

They reformed their chain. Shuffling feet and concentrated breathing once again became the norm. Those that had followed them no longer made themselves known.

"Slower, here," Minotan announced, "and beware of what's beneath your feet. The pathway is scattered with residue from feasting. Movement requires our, quietly as possible, kicking it aside."

As if on cue, Gerun's foot made contact with something easily moved to one side. Of wrong shape to be a stone, of lighter character than a rock. New encounters required progression at an even slower and more pronounced shuffling gait.

"A pause here, then," Minotan said, bringing them to another full stop. "I beg your particular quiet, please, while I engage the exit and entertain a sniff before our proceeding into and through the detour."

All but Minotan, however, audibly groaned at the sudden exposure of their dilated pupils to the glare of light that came flooding fast upon them. Minotan's startled reaction was an immediate reclosing of the portal.

"You smell the enemy?" Minotan asked nervously.

"It was the glare hurting our eyes," Gerun apologized.

"Ah, *the eyes.*" Minotan sounded greatly relieved. "My mistake. I forget you come with visuals long since discarded by my kind. Remember you, then, the direction of the exit? The way from which you saw the light?"

"Yes, of course," Gerun said. There was no forgetting it. The pain of that glare had seemed as bad as anything to which Gerun had been subjected within Mishin's tortu-chamber.

"Turn from that direction, now, please," Minotan instructed. "When the detour is opened again, you'll do better in adjusting to its light if not immediately facing into it."

Gerun turned, sensing Tyra-G already turned before him.

"Ready, then?" Minotan asked.

They all consented, and the light followed quickly.

Even tuned from the light source, Gerun found himself momentarily blinded. He blinked and blinked again.

"I smell no Mysons in the immediate," Minotan assured. "The sooner we traverse their territory, the better we will be. I've handled Mysons before, of course, but I now have you to contend with."

It was only too obvious that he considered them hindrances should any such confrontation-with-Mysons occur.

"When your eyes have adjusted, we will proceed," he said.

Gerun's eyes were adapting. However, they weren't really believing what they were seeing, constantly blinking to clear an obviously distorted vision.

Those simply *couldn't* be human bones scattered so haphazardly across the floor of the maze and extending farther back into the tunnel along which their party had shuffled. Yes, human bones! Those, the very obstacles that Minotan had warned required a sloughing to one side in the darkness.

"Bones!" Tyra-G confirmed for Gerun, obviously less reluctant than he was to identify them.

"A popular dining spot, on occasion," Minotan admitted calmly. "Mysons's worship-days bring substantial food for feasting. Now, though, it is merely catch-as-catch-can season, and most diners stay clear until more abundant times. Are we ready, then?"

"I believe so," Banic said, his hand shielding his eyes as he turned more directly toward the light.

Gerun found that by squinting he could manage fairly well. It had been a long time since he'd been subjected to the full suns of a dual day. He'd lost his mobile in dead of night. There'd been no light in his unconsciousness from the inject. He'd had but moments in the false light of castle before Mishin had rushed him below ground to the dimness of the tortu-chamber. After that, more black unconsciousness, followed by the hazy light of a cell, and the complete blackness of the maze.

He read his wrist-indicator, now visible. Eliminating his estimate of time in tortu-chamber and dungeon cell, he calculated how long they'd wandered the maze. It was longer than he'd suspected.

"This way, then," Minotan said, and he led the way from the tunnel.

Immediately, Gerun saw that it wasn't the full light of dual day to which they was exposed but to a far more substantial dimness. They'd exited into a natural grotto that sprouted pyramidal extensions from ceiling and floor, like demon's teeth in a gaping maw. The available light filtered through a distant circle that hinted the real outside world.

"The Mysons's sacred cave," Minotan identified, hurrying along. His blindness seemed little hindrance as he carefully sidestepped obstacles as if they were seen. "They bring many offerings here during worship-days, little knowing what use we make of them." He laughed an obscene sound that hinted at his kind's clever deceptions of Mysons who thought human offerings were grabbed up by unseen gods.

Tyra-G's eyes flashed disgust but, likewise, warned Gerun that it would do none of them any good to comment unfavorably upon their guide's cannibalistic appetites. Whether Minotan ate Mysons or whatever, he *was* leading *these* three beings to safety.

Minotan took them deeper into the grotto, then into a lead-off tunnel that was so low and so narrow that Gerun was scraping all sides as he squeezed through. The available light grew dimmer and dimmer, until Gerun thought they were already returned to the maze. He was wrong, though, because, when the face of the concelo sped up, the blackness beyond was of such completeness and intensity that it seemed as solid and as impenetrable as any solid wall. Automatically, Gerun's hands went to Banic's shoulders and felt Tyra-G's fingers at his waist. He steeped forward to be engulfed by deep darkness that went a hell of a lot darker once the concelo face closed behind them.

"Aaaghhhh!" Gerun groaned, lifting his left hand from Banic's shoulder.

"Gerun?" Tyra-G asked nervously from behind him.

"Problems, Missionary?" Minotan asked, having stopped their progress.

"A mere finger cramping," Gerun said. "No need to pause. I'll merely work it out while we go along, only my right hand monitoring linkage."

"Yes," Minotan agreed. "Improvisation is good, for we have much space yet left to travel."

* * * * * * *

"I SUSPECT YOU ALL NEED REST," Minotan said. How many footsteps later?

"Yes, thank-you," Banic said, his weight heavy as he slid tunnel wall to floor.

"I shall look ahead," Minotan said, sounding not in the least tired or exhausted. "I expect no difficulty, but time may be saved if I check now."

Gerun waited for the sounds of Minotan leaving, but—as usual—heard nothing. Once again, it was only his intuition that told him their guide was, indeed, gone deeper.

"By the gods, I *am* exhausted," Banic said.

"We should probably all sleep," Tyra-G said. "Hopefully to achieve energy reserves to get us out of here without too much longer in the darkness."

"Amen," Gerun agreed. He'd been hoping for ages that they could stop to sleep. Not that he was tired. Suddenly, he was too keyed up for that. He'd been nurturing a plan, since shortly after Minotan detoured them through the Mysons's worship cave, and that plan had become less and less feasible the farther they had moved back into the maze.

Gerun should have made his break before Minotan threaded them all quite so far back into the darkness. But he'd been disoriented by the light, and he'd been put off by all the legends he'd ever heard of the Mysons's barbarity toward strangers. Mysons had enslaved Jon Missionary, had they not?

If Minotan barbarity was an equal to that of the Mysons, as evidenced by the old man's relish in discussing dining, at least Minotan was an apparent ally to Gerun at this time. Minotan, Banic, and Tyra-G were simply too powerfully friendly anchors for Gerun too quickly to jettison them in an otherwise hostile environment.

Then again, Gerun's comfort with his present companions possibly dulled his wits to the reality that any rescue of him by them was possibly motivated by less than friendly incentives. Tyra-G had warned that her father might see Gerun merely as a fee to be paid for entrance through doorways in the City not normally opened for minor-noblese from a mere town. That, and not any genuine compassion for tree-connect by long-dead Rea-Cwan, was the more likely reason for Gerun's presence.

Nonetheless, Gerun *had* been lulled by Minotan's seemingly good will and by how Gerun so wanted to believe that Tyra-G and Banic were friendly tree. He didn't want to leave them and return to an existence where *he* was again the one required to decide where he was going and how he was getting there. For the moment, those decisions were made for him; Banic had a definite end-goal in mind, Minotan taking them all there. Alone, Gerun would be back, wandering a threatening landscape, without a clue as to which way to turn.

Banic's gentle snoring brought Gerun back to the here and now. To the other side of Gerun, Tyra-G's breathing was low and even. Was she sleeping, too?

If Gerun were going to leave, he would have to do it soon, if he hadn't already waited too long. Maybe opportunity had knocked, and he'd failed to open the door, because he'd been too afraid to respond. He'd been too desirous of pretending everyone was his friend.

He glanced toward the darkness through which he'd come. What if he hadn't perfectly remembered his route on the way in and would now be unable to backtrack his way out? What if there were members of Minotan's family, waiting back there with the hopes of picking up another straggler for dining? Would Gerun's efforts be rewarded by becoming one more pile of human bones among the many scattered on the tunnel floor?

What if he found the concelo, exited through it, only to confront hostile Mysons on the outside? Mysons weren't friends to anyone. They sought little contact with the outside, enslaving all who ventured in. They would have been invaded and dealt with long ago if their desolate habitat had offered even one incentive to any invader. The only thing they possessed of worth—and that of worth only to the Xeons with a stomach mutated enough for addiction to it—was suji-juice. No one but Xeons wanted suji-juice.

The Xeons, possibly powerful enough to conquer the Mysons (little was known of the Xeons except that they were addicted to suji-juice and had invented brain-blank), were rumored afraid to take

119

the chance under Mysons's threat that all suji-juice brew masters would be put to the sword before the Xeons would have them.

As it stood, exchanges of humans (mainly Xeons) for Mysons's suji-juice composed the present barter system that worked to the mutual benefit of both sides. Where a discovered Gerun would fit into that symbiotic relationship was uncertain but predictably unfavorable to him. His ancestor, Jon Missionary, hadn't fared well with either Xeons or Mysons.

Then, again, Gerun, in the wake of his present company, was presently headed back for the City. Warluck was in the City. The Religio-College was in the City. The final purge of clan Missionary might well be awaiting him in the City.

It was a case, once again, of trying to weed out the best among nothing but bad alternatives. What was there about the contentment Gerun derived from having Tyra-G beside him, though, that, once again, flooded him with conviction that it was best for him to stay right where he was?

Whatever Gerun's sense of returned contentment, Tyra-G was far wiser.

"You must go, Gerun," she said, her voice a low whisper. She hadn't been sleeping, then. "You've memorized the way back to the Mysons, yes?"

"Yes." But had he? Granted, he'd *tried* to memorize his way back to the grotto. He'd dragged his free left arm along the wall, monitoring the veerings passed without entering. He'd kept a running count, but the count had gone higher and higher. What if he'd miscounted, even once? He could end up lost forever within this maze where anyone or

120

anything confronted would see him no more or less than dinner.

"I was confused when you didn't make your move in the grotto," Tyra-G confessed, "but maybe this *is* wiser, Minotan gone. We don't know the full scope of his power, do we?"

"You're sure I wouldn't be better off taking my chances with you and your father?" He hoped she would say that, yes, it was best for him to stay.

"I truly love my father," Tyra-G said, "but he goes from top fu-dog of a town to low man on the City's totem. It won't be an easy transition for him to make. For his own good, I'd prefer you not be there to offer temptation. He would one day come to regret tree-betrayal for advancement, but the harm would already be done."

"Good-bye, then." Gerun realized that her concern for his escape was more indication of her love for her father than any feelings felt for Gerun Missionary.

"May your god go with you, Gerun Missionary," she said.

It would have been nice if she'd kissed him. That was the way it always happened in the stori-recorder tapes. However, this was reality, not fiction, wasn't it? This was no parting of lovers, but the farewell of a wanted man and a young girl, the latter not wanting her father's conscience scarred by selling tree—even distant tree—for position and profit.

Gerun left them. Hearing her audible sigh of relief in being rid of him? Or, was the sound he heard only more of Banic's snoring?

Having dragged his left arm, in, he dragged his right arm, out; his right hand was flush against the wall to recognize anything noted on his way in that needed to be noted on his way out.

The farther he retraced the darkness—alone—the more his inner senses told him he'd waited far, far, far too long. His only way out was with Minotan whom he was deserting. He'd never remember the route back to the grotto. Never.

He stopped. He was sweating but cold. He began to shiver.

Dear Jon-Missionary's God, he was so afraid!

CHAPTER TEN

"But what if there are more where this one came from? What if the next isn't made vulnerable by watria, brain-blanked by the Xeons? What if we don't get the next one before it's too late?"

"Then we either revamp our whole religio-complex to adapt to the shattering of Kanran-9 as the universal epi-center, or we see people turning against *us* as heretics. Either way, it bodes ill fortune for the Religio-College, wouldn't you say?"

"Pray it remains half-wit! Pray it comes alone! Pray it doesn't have family, friends, or fellow-travelers who'll come looking for it! Pray its god is weak!"

"Pray? Isn't that somewhat of a misnomer in the face of the evidence against us?"

—Excerpt from Recording 6i-2-4IV.
Conversation between Panrun-Ru
and Maulaus Kif.
Date: 6-4-3-2. Time: 6:2-1.
Security Clearance: FNOEBM.

HE SHOULD HAVE gone back. But, no, he'd decided going back would be a cop-out. A real man made decisions, based upon in-put, and he stuck to them. He didn't rebound back and forth, like a tennisit ball. And Gerun had analyzed his predicament and had decided he was better off away from Tyra-G, her father, and Minotan. If he didn't escape them now, he might never have another chance. No one but Banic knew what kind of greeting waited at the other end of the line possibly to clamp Gerun in chains and haul his ass off as grand prize to Warluck in the City. Tyra-G certainly had her suspicions that Gerun's chances weren't the best at the other end of the maze, or she surely wouldn't have been so anxious to send him on his separate way.

So, he'd in-put all of that, and he'd made his decision, completely overlooking the possibility that getting to the concelo wouldn't necessarily mean he could open it. He'd searched all over the wall section for the release mechanism and hadn't been able to find it. Reluctantly, he remembered how much difficulty Mishin had had in locating the release for the concelo between Gerun's room and Tyra-G's room at the castle. And, at the time, Tyra-G had already demonstrated where the catch was located. How much chance did Gerun have of finding *this* release catch if it was as cleverly concealed as that other one?

That was assuming there was even a release catch to find. He wasn't at all sure he'd successfully found his way back to the entrance of the grotto. It had been very disorienting, alone in the darkness, and—if he followed his memory mentat of veerings encountered and passed—his faculty for one-hundred-percent recall had never been the best. Why hadn't he more fully developed his mentat-capacities as he'd so often been encouraged to do so?

Again, he hand-searched the wall section and came up empty. There simply wasn't a release mechanism to be found. That left him colder, sweatier. Where did he go from here if there was no exit to be found?

The idea of screaming for help seemed unmanly. Nor could he forget Minotan's remarks about the soldiers, *meals,* left lost and screaming, *to their diners,* in the maze behind them. Gerun had no assurances that Minotan would reach him before Minotan's kin beat the old blind man to the punch (or, rather, to *lunch?*). Besides, what guarantee did Gerun have that the old man would even bother? Minotan owed Gerun nothing. The extra effort of rounding Gerun up might even, somehow, cancel out Minotan's obligations to Banic and put Banic, Tyra-G, and Gerun suddenly up for inclusion on a gourmet menu.

Where was that blasted concelo release mechanism?

He tried ritual, dropping to his knees and bruising his kneecaps on one of the many bones that continued to encourage him into thinking that he'd correctly retraced his path. However, as he remembered it, the bones stretched for a good long ways. The concelo, bones or not, could be anywhere, feet, yards, or even farther, from where he now stood.

He tented his hands beneath his chin and shut his eyes. The latter seemed a useless exercise, since it was no darker with his eyes shut than with them open. Still, ritual was ritual with prescribed steps to follow. Leave out any of the steps, and he might not make the connection. If there was really anybody there to pick up at the other end of the line.

Hold on, Gerun! This isn't the time, old buddy boy, to question the existence of Jon Missionary's god. No deity is liable to be all that receptive to someone merely mouthing words. Especially when that someone is begging for his life.

"God of Jon Missionary," Gerun began, quickly deciding that he'd better make a firmer commitment than that. "God *of mine,"* he tried. "Thank you for getting me this far with my life. Be with me that I might continue to live and spread word of your existence."

Nothing. So, what was he expecting? A bolt of ligh-nen, a roar of thu-nun, a shattering of rock and stone, an entrance to the grotto blasted out for him by some kind of celestial Cylic blazer? Maybe, he *was* expecting that.

He un-tented his fingers. He opened his eyes. He got to his feet. He surveyed the wall section, by feel, once again, his hands moving slower across surfaces this time. Maybe Jon Missionary's god was better at helping those who helped themselves. Then, again, maybe Gerun was destined to live out the rest of his life in blackness, waiting for someone or something to come along and make dinner of him, BECAUSE he still wasn't finding a release catch.

He tasted his panic; it was bitter. He felt its frantic beating inside his chest, neck, and temples. He experienced its sickening churn in the depths of his guts. No matter that his panicking wasn't going to help him one single bit.

He resorted to ritual again. If nothing else, it continued to have a calming effect on him. Without his even attempting verbally to contact Jon Missionary's God, his heartbeat slowed and his stomach ceased making quite so many somersaults. "I've really done all I can do on my own, dear God," Gerun began. "I really have tried to help myself, but I'm really going to need a little bit of assistance from You."

Still nothing. No voice from on high, telling him to move twelve feet to the right, reach six feet from the ground and two feet to the left of that for the release catch.

He struggled to his feet again, determined to keep the peaceful aura the ritual had given him—if the ritual had given him nothing else.

Had he thoroughly searched this stretch of wall with his hands and found nothing? Did it warrant additional attention, or should he methodically begin searching left and/or right of where he now stood?

Had he really believed that he'd retraced his steps *exactly*? Had he arrived, thinking the release mechanism *would* be right there? Had his confidence been nothing more than wishful thinking? Had he known from the start that his mentat-memory had never been developed to the point where it would remember as much as he'd needed it to remember?

He began to hand-search the wall section again, slowly moving his palms so that they crossed one expanse of rock surface and, then, moved back to overlap a bit of space already covered.

Nothing, nothing, nothing, but he still refused to panic. It was important that he made sure every speck of space was examined. If he didn't find anything on the wall above his head, nor down at his waist, that didn't mean that the release hadn't been triggered by the old man's knee or by his foot.

He caught his breath and, in his excitement, lost the small nodule he'd just located. He lost his cool, beginning a frantic haphazard fanning of the wall where he thought his discovery had just been made and lost. FINDING NOTHING.

Calm, calm. He needed to be calm. He prayed again, asking God to just let there be what Gerun had truly believed he'd felt there.

It took longer this time for him to achieve his calm. It took all of his willpower to begin another thorough scan of the wall section from its top to its bottom. He'd found the *thing* last time, doing it that way, and he could find it again the same way. Except what if he'd only *imagined* finding it? What if he'd only *thought* he'd felt a man-made nodule, because he'd so baldy *wanted* it to be there?

There! No. Yes. No. A bump, all right, but not the right texture. His heart sank. His surge of hope had been for nothing. The nodule he'd felt before was lower, much lower. He remembered this bump from before, remembered rejecting it and moving on. Didn't he?

Had he really dropped this far toward his knees? Had he really been this near a squat? Before?

Yes, there it was. There it exactly was. *Keep contact with it this time. Define it with fingertips.*

Natural or man-made? Could be natural. There was no point in deluding himself. On the other hand, there was something about the unseen texture of the thing, about the smoothness of the wall immediately surrounding it that....

The concelo face slid into the space above him, confounding Gerun with the full-force brilliance of light so painful that he thought himself permanently blinded.

Automatically, his hands went automatically to his face, his palms pressing against lids reflexively dropped in response to the forceful stimuli. He stumbled forward, anxious to escape the maze, even in his present state of blindness. Some release catches were possibly on timing devices. If that was the case with this one, he wanted through before the face was down again. Besides, he wasn't at all sure what he'd done to trigger the mechanism, or how he might do it again. Hell, maybe, *he* hadn't triggered it at all. Maybe Jon Missionary's God, *Gerun's* God, had been there in the tunnel with him.

His eyes continued to burn. He turned back toward the maze and its blackness. As he did so, he heard the almost silent sigh of descending concelo face.

In time—a seemingly very long time—longer than it had seemed that time Minotan had inadvertently opened the exit and exposed Gerun to painful brightness—Gerun's eyes began not to ache. The blinding flashes that had played continuously across them faded, and then dissolved completely.

Finally, he dropped his hands, waited, and then slowly opened his eyes. He expected, at the very least, sight distortion, and the light he suddenly perceived did *seem* a lot dimmer than he remembered.

He was in the tunnel at the back of the grotto. He turned slowly toward the grotto, feeling the apertures of his eyes closing father in reaction against more light.

He kneeled in ritual, this time to give thanks. After which, he squeezed through the tunnel toward freedom, taking bigger and bigger strides around the pyramidal forms sprouted from the floor and hung from the ceiling.

He rounded one massive pyramidal up-thrust and literally collided with a man in his pathway.

Gerun was slower to regroup than the Mysons. Yes, a Mysons! If Gerun had never come face to face with one before now, there had been a genetic typing on libro-recordo-indexes.

What now? Run? If Gerun had no weapon, neither, at least apparently, did the Mysons. So, perhaps, it would be better for Gerun to stand and fight. If he disabled the man, there would be less chance of word getting around that Gerun was holed up in the grotto.

His decision, though, was taken completely out of his hands. He'd no sooner estimated that he had the Mysons out-muscled and out-weighed than pain ricocheted the back of his head. As he dropped first to his knees and then forward onto his face, it struck him that just because he'd seen only one Mysons, a really on-top-of-it-all person would have had the good sense to check for the possibility of more.

Much, much later, the haze cleared momentarily from his head, long enough for him to hear snatches of conversation. If the Mysons's tongue was derived from the same language roots as Rylonian, it came complete with its own accent and vernacular that made it difficult for Gerun to understand.

"I tell you," someone said, "it's the one they want returned. Where else have you seen eyes the color of his?"

"But after so long?"

"I say we try. If they buy, then we'll know. If not, what are we out? He's powerfully built and will make someone a good slave."

So, after all, Gerun would be sold to Warluck, not by Banic but by the Mysons. He would have preferred exchanging his life for benefits to be derived by his tree. But who'd give him any farther says in the matter?

He actually welcomed the sudden return of flooding unconsciousness.

CHAPTER ELEVEN

"I never dreamed what this secret would entail."

"You *did* keep it a secret, though, didn't you, Kapo?"

"Of course."

"Good. You can see the confusion this might cause if we were to let it slip out. Explanations too complicated for just everyone."

"There *are* explanations?"

"Of course, there are explanations."

"For a man not being human?"

"You are sure of these results, then?"

"Whose body is it? Where did you get it? Where's its head?"

"I want the body incinerated. Now."

"Others should be here. Phsi-phis Morley—"

"You've said nothing to Phsi-phis Morley, have you?"

"No, but he *should* be told. Who will believe it *without* the body provided in conclusive evidence?"

"Exactly! Actually, one too many *already* knows. For which, I *am* sorry, Kapo."

"Please, no! I promise not to tell a soul."

"I'm afraid this is all too important for me to take the chance."

GERUN, THE HERETIC, BY WILLIAM MALTESE

—Expunged section of
Recordo tape 65-7R6III.

GERUN DIDN'T ASK, although asking would have undoubtedly been the fastest way to get the answers. Instead, he shut his eyes again, hoping his return to consciousness went unnoticed by the man in the room with him.

He began an admittedly confused mentat-analysis of his situation, trying to figure out for himself why he wasn't dead, where he was, and who the man with him was.

The man wasn't a Mysons. There was a distinctly wide forehead and pointed nose that was characteristic of the Mysons's gene makeup, and this man had neither. However, he had none of the distinctive Rylon characteristics, either. Somewhere in the libro-recordo-indexes Gerun had once seen, there was a genetic typing to be recognized. If only he could isolate it.

"Welcome back to the living, Gerun Missionary," the man said, and Gerun knew his unidentified companion had been just as observant as Gerun had been afraid he would be. "I wonder if you can really know how lucky you are that your Mysons captors included one who'd heard the myth song of the Xeon Drought-Causer."

Gerun opened his eyes.

"Where am I?" he asked. The same old, trite, standby question, except he didn't seem up to making deductions of his own. His head ached. "Who are you?"

"You are now moved to territory controlled by the Xeons."

"Xeons?" Gerun questioned. Yes, the man *was* Xeon.

"I am Raban-Watt, Xeon representative to the Religio-College, and presently (another happy coincidence for both of us), home on leave."

"Happy coincidence?" Gerun doubted Raban-Watt was a friend. Why should he be? He was a member of the Religio-College. Warluck headed the Religio-College. The purge of the clan Missionary, whether official or unofficial, had been conducted with, at the very least, Religio-College consent.

"*Happy,* because I've decided to handle this in a way that others might have decided less preferable than shipping you back to the City from which you've fled. My desires are to keep you for as long as it takes to dispel the dangerous cult aspects which have arisen, here, around the unfortunate passage of Jon Missionary through our territory so many terns ago. Do you realize there are some of my people who actually believe *you* are the resurrected Jon Missionary?"

Raban-Watt's robe was civilenic-wacy. Gerun should have immediately recognized its cut, except it wasn't the more official robe Gerun was used to seeing upon members of the Religio-College. Undoubtedly, on this, his home ground, Raban-Watt wore more traditionally Xeonic costumes.

"I am Gerun Missionary," Gerun said, forgetting that Raban-Watt had already told him as much. Gerun's reaction time was slowed. He had a metallic taste on his tongue that hinted of administered drugs. If a Mysons had whacked him over the head in the grotto, it would have required time to get him here. Had he been drugged all of that time?

"Of course, you're Gerun Missionary," Raban-Watt confirmed. "I know that, you know that, any one with a modicum of sense knows that. Unfortunately, there are large groups of my people who aren't with sense enough to sort out present from past, real from fake, seed from seeder. How much easier it would be had Jon Missionary not been stolen from his grave. Tell me; was that a clever plan of his wife to perpetrate the myth of his divinity?"

"Jon Missionary wasn't divine," Gerun said. Oh, he knew there were those of his clan who thought otherwise (*had* thought otherwise, anyway, while they'd been living), but the majority had never looked upon Jon Missionary as a god. "His words *told* of God."

"His words," Raban-Watt repeated with a sarcastic grimace. "His words, in total, were pure, unadulterated garble."

"Garble that survived the infamous Xeon brain-blank," Gerun bragged.

"Yes," Raban-Watt admitted. "And the clever witch Melina-Lu certainly milked that for all it was worth, didn't she? *'Words so thoroughly etched on the victim's mind that they survived even the Xeon brain-blank!'* Isn't that how she preached it?"

"How do *you* explain their survival?" Gerun challenged, coming to a sitting position. He was surprised that he wasn't fettered to the couch on which he'd been put. He was surprised to find the room apparently unguarded from within.

"An accident," Raban-Watt explained. "A foul-up in administering the brain-blank."

"When there were never flaws before?" Gerun prodded.

"There are *always* exceptions to *any* rule," Raban-Watt argued. "Although how much easier it

136

would be had there been no such exception in the case of Jon Missionary. So many coincidences have piled one upon the other to get us where we are to-day. Count them: a stranger, a failed brain-blank, a drought, a strange talisman, a clever woman, a robbed grave, a myth-song, an ignorant people... and on and on. Although it all adds up to giving you a few more minutes of life, so I can't expect you to do similar complaining."

He came closer to the couch, and Gerun tried to read something in the man's unfathomable eyes.

"But don't think, Gerun Missionary, that you've escaped the grim reaper," Raban-Watt warned. "What you've been given is only a momentary re-prieve. As soon as it becomes apparent to the igno-rant masses of my people that you're not Jon Mis-sionary returned, they will tire of you and discard their superstitions. And, it *will* be obvious—after time—that you aren't Jon Missionary. Shall I tell you why?"

"Not unless you make it plainer than what you've said so far."

"Very well," Raban-Watt conceded. "I can make it as clear as you want. Just come along with me on a short walk, a picture worth a thousand words. In that, we've put these quarters close to the heretic shrine to make it more convenient, all of the way around."

"What shrine?"

"Come," Raban-Watt insisted. "It will all be clear before too long."

Gerun shifted and swung his feet to the floor.

"Will my legs support my weight?" he asked. At the moment, he wasn't all that sure they would.

Raban-Watt looked confused for a moment.

"Oh, because of the drugs used, you mean?" he responded with sudden realization. "The narcotic residue should be quite minor by now. Little chance of any present weakness worsening."

Gerun took him at his word and successfully achieved a standing position.

"These are your liv-quarters," Raban-Watt said, waving his arms to encompass the large room they were in. "Follow, please," he beckoned and led the way to a slido-door that opened at his touch.

They exited onto a wide porch that was breeze-filled and pleasant. Within the area, large and small trays of fruit, cakes, vegetables, and other edibles, had been placed.

"Your offerings," Raban-Watt said, stooping before one laden tray and removing an aplocot which he tossed to Gerun; Gerun's coordination still wasn't what it should be, and he almost missed the simple catch. "As you can see," Raban-Watt said, "they are quite substantial at the moment. But, as of the moment, you've done nothing to disillusion the bringers, have you? I would suggest you file away the non-perishable items for those days ahead when one and all suspect you for the fraud you are and become less generous. I'd file away all liquid nourishment, for sure, because that—" He motioned toward a conlistal lake below the slope. "—is watria and not recommended. To sample it is to invite a loss of consciousness, as your ancestor Jon Missionary discovered to most everyone's avid dissatisfaction."

Raban-Watt led the way down a flight of stairs. Gerun followed, tempted by the aplocot in his hand.

He was hungry and wondered if the fruit was poison. Possibly, but it hardly seemed likely. Had Raban-Watt meant to kill him, it would have been easy, without waiting until now.

Gerun opened the fruit and savored its tart sweetness on his tongue.

They took a pathway leading to the lake. The landscape was attractive without being lush. It seemed deserted of people, except for the two of them.

"The shrubbery is deceptive," Raban-Watt said, and Gerun felt the same uneasiness he'd felt whenever grandfather Kalvin read his thoughts. Raban-Watt was the last person with whom Gerun wanted shared-mentat. "It is all watria-supported," Raban-Watt continued. "Therefore, all inedible. Don't be tempted by *any* outdoor nourishment except what's brought to you in offering."

"Brought by whom, by the way?" Gerun asked, still seeing no one.

Raban-Watt stopped for a moment and made a slow three-hundred-and-sixty-degree turn. Don't you feel their eyes on us even now?" he asked.

Gerun wasn't sure what he felt. His mind still reeled from unanswered questions as to how he'd gotten from the Mysons's grotto to Xeon's here. His body and mind were still partially dysfunctional from drug residue.

"You worshipers are merely too shy to approach," Raban-Watt said.

"Worshipers?"

"They think you are Jon Missionary returned, remember?" Raban-Watt reminded. "Word reached them, even here, that the man exchanged by us to the Mysons, and captured from the Mysons by the Rylons, was 'resurrected' from his grave. You certainly fit the myth-song recollection. Not so strange, since you share Jon Missionary's gene bank."

"Jon Missionary's body was stolen from its grave, not resurrected from it," Gerun begged to differ.

"Yes, likely so," Raban-Watt agreed. "But tell that to the foolish heretics who watch us. Convince them, and we'll soon enough be done with this charade." He smiled his smile-absent-of-all-humor. "But early endings wouldn't benefit *your* desire for life extension, so I won't expect any miraculous short-cuts."

They proceeded down the pathway, the watria sparkling its conlistal coloring beneath the dual sun.

"Of course, Xeon guards watch, too," Raban-Watt reminded. "It wouldn't do my relationship with Warluck any good to let you escape, when Warluck so strains at the bit knowing I have you. If he wasn't so involved with the Westicks's invasions, he'd not be held back from having you, despite all my protestations to persevere. So, there's yet another coincidence that has worked in your favor. Your luck seems to be on a roll. Any more superstitious a man than I might well believe you had come complete with your own protective God."

Had Jon Missionary's God brought Gerun this far? Was it purely accidental that Gerun had started out running blind and had ended up here where the first evidence of Jon Missionary had come to life?

"Sprang seemingly from nothing, your ancestor did," Raban-Watt said. "We still have the record of it, of course. Not that it was recorded on the spot.

Jon Missionary, at the time, was nothing but another find to be exchanged for suji-juice. However, witnesses were gathered later, during the Great Drought, their testimony taken. Had our security been better in those days, in those early days, preventing Jon Missionary from slipping into our territory unaware, his better-known origins would likely have better kept the ensuing legend in check. Nonetheless—" He shrugged. "—we are left to deal with what we are left to deal with."

They reached the lake's edge where slopping sounds resulted from offshore breezes blowing liquid against shoreline rocks.

"He mistook watria for liquid nourishment and suffered the numbing consequences," Raban-Watt said, obviously referring to Jon Missionary. "He was confiscated, along with his talisman; brain-blanked, as is our custom with strangers for exchange; and transported to a barter point. He made his next mumble only after actual exchange conclusion. Recognizing the obvious malfunction, we wanted him back, of course, but his buyers weren't cooperative. Jon Missionary, as your physique bears witness, was a slave to be desired. He was brain-blanked enough for the Mysons. So, they took him, leaving Xeons abuzz with conjecture as to *how* heretofore unfaultable brain-blank procedure *had* malfunctioned.

"The Great Drought commenced, if it had not begun already, and there was sudden need for the masses to understand the causes of their suffering. They were told Zzooaal was angry because of no fron-birds offered at last Mas-time, but some heretic whispered of the stranger whose mind had been stronger than brain-blank, which insinuated Jon-Missionary revenge!" He spat.

"Perhaps it was just that," Gerun ventured.

"What better proof that legend-build was crap than for us to buy back, whatever the cost, the germ-kernel himself?" Raban-Watt argued. "Putting the reality on display as the babbling half-wit he was, not as any god made angry! But, by then, the Rylons had taken him in a raid on a Mysons's encampment, twice removing him from our grasp, and Melina-Lu already had her covetous eyes on the man. How much inconvenience could still have been avoided but for the unchained lust of that slut."

Raban-Watt faced Gerun squarely, his countenance anything but friendly.

"So, here you come, thinking to avoid Warluck's net. Thinking, too, to weasel a place for you among my superstitious people? Thinking to further undermine my power base by bolstering this god of your own? Well, I welcome the day, because this will be the end of it all, finally.

"You've bought yourself only a few precious moments more, not a lifetime. Why? Because, those same superstitious fools who have, over the years, elevated Jon Missionary so close to heretical-god-state, likewise credit him with the Empass. Thinking you are Jon Missionary resurrected, they assume you to have the key to penetrate. In failing penetration, you will discredit the legend, dethrone the false god, and deem yourself heretic in the bargain. For that reward, I can only thank you, not condemn you, for coming."

"What is this *Empass*?" Gerun asked. Did he really know anything of what Raban-Watt was saying? Was it really true that Jon Missionary's ideas of a new god had somehow been left here as well as transported with him, distorted here by an ignorant populace who confused the messenger with the god? Not so fantastic a premise when thinking of how several clan members, of more high intelligence than commonplace Xeons, had believed Jon Missionary god rather than prophet. Whether prophet or god, the heresy threatened the Religio-College, and Warluck sought to purge it.

"Anxious, are you, for Empass?" Raban-Watt asked sarcastically. "No more anxious than I am for you to have at it."

He led the way up a pathway, not the one back to the house, not the one to the lake, but another that meandered through rocks and trees. Beyond the trees, there was a sandy stretch without growth.

"The way to XXex," Raban-Watt said. "It was sand well-traveled in ancient time. Well-traveled until Empass time. Who knows the cause of Empass? Magno-electrice *beneath* Kanran-9 crust. Or, mango-electrice *within* Kanran-9 heavens. The Religio-College agrees. For, though Empass is said to have appeared in Jon Missionary's time, it's highly suspected that time-lapse has merely caused that misinterpretation. Undoubtedly, it was Empass long before Jon Missionary, or long after him. If the two *did* occur simultaneously, it was but another coincidence of many. Jon Missionary did not walk the path and then proceed to seal it with Empass in preparation for his return. I guarantee it. As does the Religio-College."

"I see no visible mystery in this," Gerun said. "A sandy knoll. Ascending layers of dune. Aborted path at the edge of the sand. A spot unseeded by even watria-thriving growth."

"Walk farther with me," Raban-Watt said. "No time like the present to begin. See how eagerly the heretics wait?" He pointed, and Gerun's gaze was quick enough to see watching faces disappear behind stands of distant boulders.

"What is this place?" Gerun asked, encouraged that, despite all the talk, Raban-Watt seemed little afraid of proceeding.

"Empass, as I've already said," Raban-Watt said. "A wonder instigated by Jon Missionary upon his passage through, or so the faulty saying goes. I've told you my opinion, and the official opinion, on the matter of origin."

Gerun was prepared to ask for more specifics, when he was made aware of Empass without the asking. Empass was the invisible cloyingness of atmosphere that was suddenly full about him. It was a jell unseen that slowed his walk until he was forced to pause altogether within it.

"Empass!" Raban-Watt pronounced. The force that stopped Gerun and him didn't impede their breathing or conversation. Movement was still possible backward and to the sides. Not forward.

"But...," Gerun began, but was halted by a signal by Raban-Watt to be silent.

Gerun, then, heard the alien sounds, coming from seemingly nowhere. He couldn't decipher them, except the final utterance of the series that seemed somehow very familiar.

"*Romans*," Gerun repeated. "A Jon-Missionary sound!" he exclaimed in sudden revelation.

144

"Save your game-playing for ignorant fools," Raban-Watt warned, visibly angry.

"I say *Romans* is *his* sound," Gerun insisted. "Recorded and passed down to me and mine."

"Then, make reply," Raban-Watt challenged. "Save yourself and rally these poor watching slobs, to the back and sides of us, by unlocking the Empass your founder has locked and left locked.

Raban-Watt was obviously waiting, but for what? Did he expect Gerun to come up with some magical incantation to shatter the Empass barrier and let them through? Quite the opposite. Raban-Watt luxuriated in his knowledge that Gerun Missionary, heretic, had arrived *without* the proper key. Had there been a key to the Empass, had it been used by Jon Missionary to lock the space, that key was lost with the man who turned it. Raban-Watt knew that. Before long, the watchers would know that, too. Jon Missionary was *not* back from the grave!

"The very same fools who have elevated your kin to occult status will soon enough be disillusioned by your inability to penetrate Empass," Raban-Watt prophesied. "They'll tire of bringing you food and liquid nourishment. When they're through with you, when I have need of you no longer, then Warluck will have you. Enjoy your respite while you have it, Gerun Missionary, heretic."

The alien sounds began again, an obvious repetition of what had been broadcast before. Some kind of question being asked? With hope of receiving an answer?

"Christian!" Gerun shouted response. Was not Christian that word received from the Jursimmic

Priest when Kalvin had endangered his soul by entering the Labyrinth of Klint?

Raban-Watt's face scowled with worry. But when the invisible jell of Empass wasn't released, he laughed with malicious relief.

"Do you know how close you came, just then, to having another believer?" Raban-Watt asked guiltily. "Unfortunately, you've missed your chance for this convert. Soon, you will have used up all of your chances. *Christian,* indeed." He laughed again. "Good show, my boy. Not, I'm afraid, good enough, however."

He did a quick about-face and headed back the way he had come.

Gerun checked the Empass jell again, finding it no more prepared to let him through than it had before.

From wherever, the mumbled of Jon Missionary sounded again, asking what question, expecting what answer from Gerun?

From behind him, and to each side, fanatical eyes watched—and waited.

CHAPTER TWELVE

"In retrospect. Of course, in retrospect. But how could we possibly have foreseen it then?"

"Do you know it's whispered even the Xeons have a cult to this man, the heresy now enforced by gossip of his resurrection?"

"So the Xeon's august member of the Religio-College has so complained often enough."

"If only it were possible to put the body back, we might squelch the absurdities."

"Unfortunately, as you now know, the body is incinerate and beyond recovery."

—Excerpt 14-6-6VI.
Conversation between Samtol-Mu VI and
Samtol-Mu VII (AKA Roger Sorrento).
Date: 56-6-4-3. Time: 6:3:4-6.
Security Clearance: FNOEBM.

THEY WERE STONING his liv-quarters again. Aiming from closer than before, by the sounds of the thuds, too. Someone had even gotten up the gumption to throw a stone at Gerun, himself, the other day, although that disappointed pilgrim was—luckily for Gerun—still the exception to the rule. Not that Gerun could blame them. They were simple people, after all. Few, if any of them, had much education to speak of. They'd found something in the Jon-Missionary legend upon which to focus their beliefs, and now Gerun's inability to penetrate Empass had them questioning their beliefs. They felt as if they'd been betrayed by the god to whom they'd devoted so much time and energy. That Jon Missionary had never been a god, that Gerun Missionary was not Jon Missionary resurrected, was a hard lesson to take for people whose parents and grandparents had been born and had died under the illusion that Empass was Jon-Missionary locked and could be Jon-Missionary unlocked.

Raban-Watt, of course, was delighted by the way things progressed. He'd stopped by just the day before to boast how Gerun's time was quickly running out. If Warluck wasn't so much involved with fighting the Westicks, Raban-Watt would have probably been forced to turn Gerun over to the Religio-College way before now. However, Warluck's energies *were* still temporarily channeled elsewhere, so Raban-Watt saw every advantage in keeping Gerun around a while longer, until *all* heretics—far and wide—were convinced, once and for all, that Gerun Missionary (AKA *the resurrected* Jon Missionary to the ignorant fools) had no real power in overcoming Empass.

Even Gerun was beginning to wonder why he daily went through the routine. It was probably egotistical of him to believe he *had* somehow come with the key to the illusive lock. It was simply flattering for him to believe that he'd somehow been guided to this place by a greater force than his own. It was satisfying to see himself as a tool for Jon Missionary's God, saved from Warluck, from the maze, from the Mysons, from the Xeons, to arrive here, on the shores of a watria lake, where the legend of Jon Missionary had begun. It hinted of mystical conclusions, a circle finally completed, the first and the last Missionary—except, hopefully, for Kalvin, of course, who, if dead, hadn't released a mentat-disturbance that Gerun's sensitivities had yet recognized.

However, even Gerun's wildest fantasies of purpose were hard to sustain when he was faced with humiliating failure, day after day after day. He wasn't so thick-skinned that some of the screamed gibes didn't affect him. When the rocks were thrown, more and more often these days, he feared their contact, knowing it was soon to come.

Maybe, he should just remain inside, today, not bothering to make the walk to Empass, there only to fail again. Just let Raban-Watt come and get him, ship him off to Warluck. Let Gerun join his clan members in the happy hereafter that Jon Missionary had somehow promised without having ever uttered a decipherable sound.

Yet, even as he contemplated not going, he knew that he would go today as he'd gone every day since Raban-Watt had first subjected him to Empass. Because somewhere deep inside of him, there was the undeniable sensation that he was there for a purpose, that he *did* have the key to Empass, if he only knew how to draw that key from within himself.

Romans? Romans? The alien question always ended with that particular sounding. Yes, a question, just by the way it was voiced, leaving that certain something hanging, unsaid, at the ending, just begging for reply. But who or what was *Romans*? As far as Gerun remembered, *Romans* was just one more mumbled word, of so many mumbled words, that had been passed down over the terns as having escaped Jon Missionary's mouth at one time or another during the man's lifetime.

Gerun mentat-concentrated, reviewing the litanies and incantations he'd committed to memory in youth: Joram, Ahaziah, Athaliah, Joash; Caesarea, Philippi, Hermon, Tabor, Galilee; Galatians, Ephesians, Timothy, One, Two, Titus.

Each time the voice had asked its question, Gerun had thrown back a reply.

As Christian hadn't been the key, nor had Edrei, nor had Egypt.

How many of those undecipherable soundings of Jon Missionary had Gerun tried, only to find the Empass as immovable as it always was? What gut feeling told him that the password was still inside him?

Even if Jon Missionary *had* ever had the key, what chance was there it had survived the rigors of Xeon brain-blank? Or, if it had survived that, who was to say it hadn't been distorted by terns of being passed from one generation to another, from one re-cordo-disc to another: Sarimah, becoming Saree-mah, becoming Sareesshama, becoming Sarah? Had Gerun, never a master of mentat-exercises, ever really had all those sounds correctly committed to memory? How futile to be spitting out answers, now, that would never be recognized because they had been memorized incorrectly in the first place!

He swung his legs over the edge of the couch and assumed a sitting position. He was dizzy, not from drugs but from hunger and thirst; his tongue was dry. He wasn't getting nearly enough liquid and nourishment. As Raban-Watt had predicted, the bringers had become less and less generous as Gerun's performance had become less and less satis-factory.

There was another clunk of another stone hitting another part of the outside of his liv-quarters. Time to chase the hecklers away. Time to check for new offerings on the porch. He hoped some die-hard had decided not to lose faith quite yet, leaving Gerun a swallow of liquid or bite of nourishment. Gerun's supply, brought into the liv-quarters from better times, was running so low he was afraid to eat and drink from it, lest he completely deplete it.

He walked to the slido-door, pausing to combat the accompanying dizziness. What if he went out there today and the rock-throwers didn't go away? What if they aimed their missiles more accurately, this time directly at him? Would Raban-Watt lose bonus points by turning Gerun's dead body over to Warluck? Probably not. Getting Gerun dead would merely save Warluck the bother of killing him.

151

Gerun touched the slido-door release, and the door opened for him. Too bad the Empass didn't oblige him as easily.

He came to his full height, threw back his shoulders, threw out his chest, and stepped outside.

A rock clunked at his feet, bounced, thereafter, to shatter a small vase of liquid nourishment. The drink splattered to waste, and Gerun could only watch helplessly. If he'd only been a second sooner, the liquid might have been saved.

Furious, he turned toward the thrower, but the thrower was nowhere to be seen. Thank God, they still retained a certain fear of him. He thanked Jon Missionary's gene bank for having delivered him of a physique that was truly impressive compared to Xeon musculature which had been bred to less-than-awe-inspiring stature. If they tried anything funny, Gerun could still break a few heads.

Ah, an aplocot. A small tray of them. He knelt for them before they, too, could be destroyed. He opened one, enjoying the refreshing squirt of its sour-sweet taste over his tongue. Mentally, he thanked the pilgrim who'd held out enough hope to keep this fakir nourished one more day. Gerun was tempted to open another of the fruit, but he decided against it. His thirst was quenched enough for the moment. Perhaps, when he returned from Empass, he would indulge himself with another. He took the tray into the liv-quarters for its contents' safety.

The Empass. Why did he continue to bother with it? Liquid refreshment and aplocots could be stretched farther if he didn't subject himself to the heat outside. What was there that kept telling him this would be the day the question would be asked and see him with the answer?

Matthew...*Romans*. Sounds somewhere in between. To the Epistles? Of what long-ago phrase or passage was he thinking? Matthew, something, something, something, To the Epistles, *Romans*. Important? Probably not.

He would have another aplocot. He opened it, his mouth collapsing around the fruit. Liquid squeezed. Guiltily, he savored the resulting pulp and moisture.

He walked back onto the porch, closing the slido-door behind him. He walked the steps, took the pathway to the watria lake. How inviting that numbing liquid looked. How deceptive a prize for someone as thirsty as Jon Missionary conceivably must have been.

Watria lapped at Gerun's feet. He stooped and ran his fingers through it. He cupped his palm, watching the way the fluid, like water, molded the contours of his hand. He could raise his cupped palm and drink from it. Jon Missionary had done as much. Gerun's unconscious body would then become as vulnerable to consequences as Jon Missionary's had been.

Matthew, Mark, John, To the Ephesians, *Romans*. No. That wasn't right.

He drained the watria between his fingers, came to his feet, and turned to the pathway leading up through the trees and rocks to the ascending dune.

Where was grandfather Kalvin? Dead? Alive? Hiding? Would Kalvin know the answer to the asked question? Would Kalvin be able to summon whatever mentat-concentration was necessary to *sense* the meaning of the question, and *sense* the proper response?

From behind the boulders, early-morning watchers watched. Not as many as there'd once been. Nor were those who remained as easily cowed. They watched, almost defiantly, hostility where once there had been expectation. Gerun was there to disappoint, and they were furious with him for it. But what could he do? They'd made him something he wasn't. Why should he pay for their ignorance and misplaced superstitions?

He felt the Empass jell begin its hold on his legs and arms. He was forced by it to a stop. He could actually lean forward and be supported by it.

What did he want beyond this Empass, anyway? What answers were there in the sand? He laughed at the ridiculousness of it. He was still laughing when the question was asked.

"Sarah," he answered, realizing he'd used the answer before. He was duplicating effort. And what if it wasn't *any* word the question demanded? What if it desired a *series* of words? A sentence, a paragraph, a chapter, a verse, composed of a language Gerun didn't know and could never know.

The Empass remained. The question was repeated. Turning his head left and right, Gerun saw the watchers watch his failure. How disgusted and/or disappointed they looked. Did they know that he would give them the performance they wanted if he could? But how could he give it? He wasn't a god. He wasn't a prophet. He wasn't Jon Missionary returned. He was Gerun Missionary, mere boy.

"Matthew-Mark," he said. Had he answered that before, too? He should have devised a better program for submission in order to avoid duplications. Instead, he'd plunged in haphazardly, as usual, picking words at random: Christ, Jerusalem, Zoram, Alma.... Now, he was probably definitely repeating. These last few days, his mind had wandered.

Whether he'd used Matthew-Mark before, it wasn't working. The Empass jell still held.

So, what other of Jon Missionary's mumbles had Gerun mentat-recorded and not fed this voice in the wilderness? *Israel?* He'd used Israel. *Holy?* He'd used Holy. *Moses?* He'd used Moses. *Zarephath?* Had he used Zarephath? He couldn't remember. No harm, he guessed, in trying it again. He had nothing else to do at the moment.

He waited for question repeat. Overdue, wasn't it? Or was his state of mind distorting time lapse? Was there a tension in the air, or was he imagining it? Were his watchers shifting nervously, or no more than usual?

He would answer the question with Zarephath. So, why wasn't the question asked? It *should* have been asked, yet again, by now.

Had he triggered Empass release? No. Wishful thinking, that. The jell still held. He could move backward, and he could move to either side. But not forward. Empass remained firm. But *something* had happened.

He counted, slowly. He'd once counted to twenty between incorrect answer and question repeat. He counted to twenty now. Nothing. He counted to twenty again. Again, nothing.

What now?

"Zarephath," he said. Maybe the question had been asked without his hearing. Maybe the mechanism had tired of asking, knowing it was wasting its time. "one…two…three—nineteen…."

The question was asked.

"Zebedee," he answered.

He counted, one to twenty.

The question was repeated. He heard it this time. He'd heard it the time before. But there had been a longer-than-usual pause in there somewhere. He hadn't imagined it. He hadn't.

"Matthew-Mark," he said. Forget Zarephath. Forget Zebedee. Matthew-Mark had triggered the pause, if Gerun could hope ever to believe an answer had triggered anything. More likely, a malfunction at the other end. A slipping of the gears. A speck of dirt momentarily caught in the delivering mechanism.

He counted to twenty. He counted to forty. He counted to sixty. Nothing.

Yes, the watchers recognized the anomaly. There were more watchers drawn by the occasion, too, with ears straining to hear a question presently on hold. Did, this mean…?

Gerun didn't have the foggiest what it meant. What it *didn't* mean was that he'd found the key to unlock Empass. As before, Empass still blocked him.

What now?

For one, the watchers were on the move. Slowly, they were emerging from behind the boulders. Rocks for stoning in their hands? No, their hands were empty. They were advancing like shy children. He wished they'd keep their distance. They were obviously expectant, and he couldn't promise them anything. He was uncertain, himself, what and how he'd given them this much.

"Luke-John," he gave additional response before the question returned.

Where *was* the question?

Gerun breathed a sign of relief when the watchers stopped all forward movement before they were within stoning distance. They looked agitated but silent. They looked apprehensive but expectant.

Who were these Xeons that they expected some kind of miracle from a foreigner? Why was Gerun even here? Why couldn't he have been allowed to live his life in peace, without the stigma of Jon Missionary hanging over his head? Why did Warluck initiate the purge of clan Missionary in Gerun's lifetime?

"The Epis!" he screamed, determined to bring the question back into being. Or, was he? Why *The Epis?* Why not Zarephath again, since *that* had already once coaxed a repeat of the question?

Matthew-Mark, Luke-John, The Epis, and.... And what? *Come on, Gerun, you had it there, subconsciously, for a moment, mentat-sorting through the mind.* A once-heard word sequence had been recalled, hadn't it? Matthew-Mark, Luke-John, The Epis....

"The Epis*tle*."

He was sweating. His heart was beating loudly. He fought back the thrill that told him he'd stumbled, somehow, upon *something*. More likely, the questioning mechanism had malfunctioned. No more question ever to be asked, and not because Gerun had said anything to silence it. He was deluding himself into thinking this was any kind of breakthrough. Was the Empass any the less resistant? No. It was as firm in its resolve against him as it had ever been.

Look at the watchers watching. They thought he was on the verge of something, too. What did they know? They were ignorant, superstitious fools. They'd elevated Jon Missionary to cult status, because they thought he'd caused their Great Drought. *Jon-Missionary vengeance,* they'd called it. For being brain-blanked. For being sold into slavery in exchange for six qall-quats of suji-juice.

How *did* the litany go? What about *The Romans? About* them, or….

"*To* the Romans,*"* he said, more to himself than to the silenced questioner. More to himself than to the watchers who watched so expectantly.

He'd been leaning forward, and the weight of his body suddenly carried forward. He was made uncoordinated by his surprise. He tripped and went down.

He heard the massive and collective intake of breath from the watchers. He scrambled to see them approaching and, in automatic response, he backed away from them. There was something about the sudden glazed quality of their eyes that he found disconcerting.

He backed farther away from them, stopping only when they stopped. With difficulty, he realized they were no longer moving only because they *couldn't* move any closer. The faces of those in the front line were flattened as if pressed firmly against a sheet of clear plexi-plast. They were held in check by Empass, in front, and by more watchers, pressing in on them from the rear.

But Gerun was somehow beyond them and beyond Empass.

A question was asked. Not of Gerun this time
but of the watchers. Gerun had already answered
and was inside.

He turned to a loud grating sound, seeing the
hole in the dune open before him.

He dropped to his knees in ritual, giving thanks,
praying for salvation, begging for the strength and
fortitude to face whatever would come forth from
the sand to claim him. He prayed for a removal of
his overpowering fear.

CHAPTER THIRTEEN

"Rylons have beaten Westicks today, but all but one have lost the bigger, more important battle waged for far greater stakes!"

—Warluck Rieege, upon hearing,
after the decisive Battle of
Sarentogotown, that Gerun
Missionary had penetrated Empass.

WHEN GERUN STOOD, he noticed that the majority of the watchers had dropped to their knees to mimic his ritual. He wondered if they received the same calming effect from it that he did. Because he was calmer, less fearful, more prepared to meet his fate within the sand.

He turned from the watchers and walked toward the opening shielded by a fine sheet of sand that waterfalled it. He had a firm sense of purpose, an unshakable belief that something mightier than he had brought him here. Why, or for what purpose, wasn't yet as clear to him, but he had no doubts but that both soon would be.

He stepped through the tumbling sand, feeling the grains on his hair and splattering down his back. He stepped upon something solid that immediately lit the darkness. He found he was on the first step of a stairway. When he placed his weight upon the second step, it lit from within, like the first one.

He was drawn upward by the same inexplicable force which had fortified him to brave the sand-cascaded hole in the first place.

When he reached the last step, it wasn't only it that illuminated. A whole wide expanse was suddenly bathed in warm glow, revealing not a cavern hollowed out of the sand by natural forces but a man-made interior filled with man-made things. And what a man-made wonder it was to behold.

He stood on the threshold of a space that had to account for a large section of the dune seen from the outside. Around him, there were machines that blinked multi-colored lights, some of their colors ones he'd never before seen. There were strange sounds, too: hums, buzzes, whirs, whatevers.

He tried to take mentat-stock of what he saw. It had an order to it that was definitely man-planned. On the other hand, Gerun could recall never having seen anything quite like it. Had he been quizzed to put names and/or functions to anything present, he would have been at a loss to do so.

He stepped deeper into the enclosure, pausing before containers that could have been neatly stacked boxes, except they looked made of no material Gerun had ever seen. And inside the boxes…?

He reached for and retrieved one of the books. And such a book he'd never before seen, either. Even in the libro-archive, where he'd seen full evidence of what had been Kanran-9 books before the introduction of recordo-units, he'd never come across the likes of this.

It was bound in a strange black substance, stiff but pliable, a wondrous golden emblem, like two crossed bars, embossed on its cover. And the pages! What marvels they were to the sight and to the touch: thin and white, except for the black runes that cluttered all but their margins.

A book like the talisman carried by Jon Missionary and gone incinerate by Panrun-Ru? Yes, but not just *one* of them. Boxes of them.

Keeping the treasure in hand, Gerun moved deeper into the room, drawn to what looked like a couple of rest-cylinders against a far wall. Except, like everything else around him, these mechanisms were like sleep-units he'd never seen duplicated before. The lid of the one, pulled up, was of seemingly thick plexi-plast. The container itself was constructed as part of the wall that curved to form the dome ceiling above it.

Gerun stopped, his fingers grasping the book tighter. The thick plexi-plast-like material of the second sleep-cylinder-like unit, the closed unit, was cracked. A web-like pattern was traced upon its surface, from head to foot, masking, but not completely, the contents.

Gerun's senses whirled. He leaned against one of the unidentified machines for support. He took strange comfort from the book he'd carried with him from its box. It gave him strength to muster the courage to retake the few steps separating him from the crack-striated surface. Beneath the damaged view-shield was a human skeleton.

What was this place, then? A tomb? The fear that he'd violated sacred ground sent his mind reeling. He stepped back, turned away, but knew his legs weren't up to taking him anywhere. He collapsed onto a contoured surface that might, or might not, be a chair. He'd certainly seen no chair of similar design.

He tried mentat-calm, surprised at how successful he was in achieving it. He reasoned it couldn't be a tomb if Jon Missionary had been alive when exiting it. And there was evidence to support Jon Missionary having once been there. For one, the open rest-cylinder. For two, the question asked in Jon Missionary's language. For three, the key which was but a sequence mumbled at one time by Jon Missionary and recorded by Melina-Lu.

But if this place wasn't as tomb, then what was it? Liv-quarters?

When he shifted for a better survey of the massive room, his chair shifted with him, turning on a center of gravity that made it convenient for Gerun to face the nearest machine.

Gerun transferred the book to his left hand and fingered one of the buttons on the machine panel before him. He wondered what sequence of events he could put into motion by each movement of but one switch. Would he blow the place and him up with it? Had he escaped death along the way, only to self-destruct, here and now? Had Jon Missionary and his dead companion (mother? father? wife? lover? brother? sister?) construct this bomb, and then protect it, all beneath the noses of the Xeons? How?

How could it possibly be here at all? How could the Xeons not have known of its construction? How could the Xeons have so long been kept from it? What power was there here, what power within Jon Missionary's control, that the man had been so able to isolate this space for so long without even being here?

Nor was it just the Xeons who'd been kept from it. Raban-Watt had insinuated that even the Religio-College knew of Empass. All the technology of the Religio-College, then, hadn't done them any good in breaking through, where Gerun had managed penetration with mere Missionary words. Could Jon Missionary have controlled such power, yet so easily been victimized by watria numbness, Xeon brain-blank, and Mysons slavery? A man so strong, yet so weak?

What secrets of Jon Missionary were here for Gerun to find? Had Gerun been somehow guided here to find those secrets, or to destroy them with the flip of one switch? Whatever, this *was* his destiny!

He activated the mechanism he was fondling. Automatically, he shut his eyes, expecting disintegration but saved from it.

He opened his eyes to the buzz of a viewing screen. A picture showed him happenings outside. Watchers in ritual pose. Other watchers bringing offerings of edibles and liquid nourishment that they were aligning along the Empass barrier. Gerun would have an abundance of food and drink again. He'd satisfied their need for grand performance.

His curious fingers moved to another dial on the same control panel. He was more brazen after his initial success. If there was the risk that he might yet blow up everyone and everything, sometimes risks had to be taken. Surely, he'd not come all of this distance, through all of his hardships, to find all of these secrets, without being given the time to unravel them. How to unravel them, if not to explore the functions of each and every dial, switch, device, lever, and mechanism?

He turned the dial one clock-click to the right. The picture on the viewing screen dissolved, the watchers and their activities erased and were replaced by something else. But replaced by what?

Gerun sat back and attempted to mentat-concentrate on what he might be seeing. The inky black backdrop, punctuated with pinpoints of light, at first appeared to be the night-sky, but there was something noticeably curious about the perspective from which it was being seen. More as if Gerun were moving through that sky, rather than looking up at it. Absurd! To be where Gerun imagined he was would have demanded higher fight than a mobile, or a Bockwin, or even a servo-ten unit. No man flew that high. No recordo-cam, either.

And what pinpoint was that, enlarging to marble size? What globe of what material? Suspended how and within what? Gerun suspected the marvel to be of the machine's making. But of what purpose such a complicated illusion?

The marble grew larger, appeared to be a moon. But no moon Gerun had ever seen. Not Moon Myl, or Moon B. Not Mithras Moon.

The moon was left behind. Up ahead, another pinpoint swelled toward expansion, as if suddenly being approached from afar.

"Ahhhh!" Gerun gasped in pleasure, caught suddenly unaware by the emerging details of the expanding light-point. For not only was it a colorful sphere, spinning like a top, but it was encircled by wondrous rings.

He sat back in his chair, more intuitively confident that it was a chair.

What a marvelous machine he had activated. What miniature models had been utilized to program such fantasies as it was relaying? By concentrating on the screen, Gerun had a definite sense of flying that was more intense than he'd experienced in any mobile. Here, he actually could believe he had left Kanran-9's gravity. What madness.

Ringed globe was replaced by another wonder: a speck in the darkness that expanded, as Gerun watched, into a largeness that filled the total screen with impossible colors that swirled upon a spherical surface. Then, that, too, was gone.

166

What next? Which dot to expand now? That one? That one? Ah, yes, *that* one. The delicate, vein-latticed red one. Not as wondrous as the ringed one, not as overpowering as the large one, but a beauty to behold, nevertheless. As if it were a fragile bubble suspended momentarily within a fine net of strings as Gerun moved passed it.

He turned from the screen, wishing to assure himself that he was land-bound. The sensation of flying so high and wild was so real to him that he'd actually thought, there for a silly moment, that he actually did it. He laughed at the ease with which he'd been tricked by the machine-produced phenomena. The room beneath the dune was still anchored firmly to Kanran-9. Listening carefully through the other noises, Gerun could even hear the sand which still waterfalled the downstairs' doorway. And a quick click of the dial to the left brought back a picture of watchers still piling offerings along the Empass wall.

Reassured, Gerun clicked back to the mysteriously appearing and disappearing globes. This time, the expanding pinpoint was blue. Blue as Gerun's eyes were blue. Blue and partly veiled by moving wisps of expander-creamer white.

There was a sudden veering in the camera angle at the exact moment Gerun expected the blue globe to swing out of focus. Instead, the pathway of filming was bent into a downward helix that circled and re-circled the blue sphere, penetrating its diaphanous white cover, and bringing everything into greater magnification.

Gerun was undeniably fascinated. From pin-point to blue marble, to large globe, to something more magnificent in close-up.

Huge seas? Of what? Watria? Liquid nourishment? Water? Land masses? It was like coming toward Kanran-9 from high in the air, except this wasn't Kanran-9. Nowhere on Kanran-9 were there such massive seas. Nowhere. Not even Gran Sea.

Lower dropped the recordo-cam, skimming the great pools of liquid, skimming the great masses of land.

And what were those? Cities? Aye, cities, but like no cities Gerun had ever seen before. What new trickery was the machine working? What artist of miniatures had so skillfully modeled these fantasies to make them seem so real?

The approach speed slowed, stalling above a meadow of green. Where on Kanran-9 had the artist found inspiration for such green?

The recordo-cam view bobbed, showing a tilted viewing of what? The interior of the ship. A man, sitting where Gerun was now sitting. For a moment, Gerun thought his image was being picked up by some cleverly hidden and activated recordo-cam. Except it wasn't him. It was....

Jon Missionary mugged for the camera, laughed, waved the cameraman away.

The filming followed a pathway to the lower stairway that automatically lowered. It exited to the outside where Gerun expected to see watchers piling offerings against Empass wall. What he saw, instead, was a strange house, people spilling from the door of it and rushing toward him. Nor were they stopped by Empass. They came all of the way to the recordo-cam.

For a moment, the viewing was confused, as if cameraman stood in place and twirled. Then, the picture again focused, and Gerun found himself looking upon a saucer-shaped object sitting in the meadow. Yet, even as he watched, the saucer began to rise and disappear into the sky with a swiftness that was startling.

Gerun switched off the machine, hardly believing what he'd seen. His mind needed time to adjust to what had seemed so real but had to be merely machine trickery. His mentat-mind had read the insinuations of other planets and other people, and that was too fantastic to believe.

Yet, what place was this he was in? Who was the skeleton in the damaged rest-cylinder? From where had Jon Missionary gotten his blue eyes? From where had the material come for the binding and the pages of the book still held in Gerun's hand? Why had Panrun-Ru deemed the book heretical and demanded it incinerate? Why the purge of the clan Missionary?

According to all the religious teachings of all the gods within the Religio-College pantheon, Kanran-9 was the universal epi-center. It, and it alone, held the lone distillation of life within an otherwise dead universe that revolved round it. There was no life but Kanranian life, and Kanranian life and Kanranian gods were Kanranian-bound.

Had Jon Missionary's arrival with his book hinted otherwise? Had Panrun-Ru sensed the danger to Religio-College gods who were suddenly threatened with competition from a god come out of the vastness?

From where was Gerun getting such wild thoughts? He was jumping to too many unproven conclusions in way too short a time. It needed more study. This place needed more study.

This book—he caressed the binding of the volume in his hand, running his fingers gently over the golden image of crossed bars embossed upon the black—needed more study.

He opened the book, seeing more of the runes he couldn't understand, now determined that he *would* understand them. He was confident he'd been drawn here with no other purpose but *to* understand them.

Penetrating the Empass had given him protection and time. If no one had broken Empass before, it was highly unlikely anyone would soon follow. Therefore, he was isolated from his enemies in a way he'd never hoped to achieve on Kanran-9. He'd gather up the offerings of edibles and liquid nourishment from the supplies being piled along the Empass barrier, and he would have subsistence within his fortress to survive. He must be sure to stockpile lots of liquid nourishment, because Jon Missionary had left this place for watria mistaken for potable drink. Gerun couldn't leave until he was better armed against his enemies beyond the barrier. His real enemies not numbness-producing watria, not brain-black Xeons, not slaver Mysons, but fiss-wielding members of the Religio-College.

What did the writing in this strange book mean? What secrets did it hold for him? What magic?

170

GERUN, THE HERETIC, BY WILLIAM MALTESE

Gerun was good at Fin-rick codes. He was an expert at the Fin-rick-code game. He'd break this cipher in time, decode all of its secrets. He was sure of it.

Then, by the God of clan Missionary, Warluck and all his land-bound gods of Kanran-9 would have even more cause to tremble with fear on their shaky and rotting foundations!